Critics rave about Simon Brett and his Charles Paris mysteries:

"Brett knows the British stage inside out, and backgrounds are unusually authentic."
—Newgate Callendar,
The New York Times Book Review

"QUITE SIMPLY THE BEST IN THE BUSINESS."
—*Kirkus Reviews*

"Solid entertainment. . . . Brett's insider's knowledge of show business . . . makes his witty mysteries go."
—*Time*

"Simon Brett, the Laurence Olivier of the theatrical mystery, writes thrillers that play wonderfully: the dialogue is witty and natural, the characterization engagingly complex, and the plots most cunningly constructed."
—*Booklist*

STAR TRAP
Simon Brett

A DELL BOOK

Published by
Dell Publishing Co., Inc.
1 Dag Hammarskjold Plaza
New York, New York 10017

Dell ® TM 681510, Dell Publishing Co., Inc.

ISBN: 0-440-18300-6

Reprinted by arrangement with Charles Scribner's Sons
Printed in the United States of America
April 1986

10 9 8 7 6 5 4 3 2 1

WFH

*To my Parents, with thanks
for all that education*

*And with special thanks to
Bill and Chris, who know
all about it*

PART 1

London

One...

'ACTUALLY,' SAID GERALD Venables, after a sip from his wine glass, 'there's a bit more to it than that.'

'Ah,' said Charles Paris. 'I thought there might be.'

Gerald took a long pause and twiddled the stem of his wine glass. Charles wondered what the catch would be. Gerald was a good friend but was unlikely to be offering him a job from purely altruistic motives. And if it were just a gesture of goodwill, he wouldn't have made it over lunch at Martinez.

'In fact,' the solicitor picked out his words like a philatelist handling stamps, 'there may be something rather odd going on in this show.'

'Odd?'

'Well, as you know, a West End musical is a very large financial undertaking and with any large financial undertaking there are probably as many people who wish it to fail as succeed. And the ... people whom I represent are very anxious that this particular show should succeed.'

'You mean you've got money in it?' Charles knew this would make Gerald bridle. Though well known in theatrical circles as a speculator, the solicitor would never admit to his involvement.

'One of the people whom I represent,' came the frosty professional reply, 'has a considerable financial stake in the venture. It is on his behalf that I am approaching you.'

Charles winked. Gerald deflated, smiled and moved

the conversation away from money. 'Listen, Charles, the reason that we want you in the show is that we need an investigator on the spot to keep an eye open for anything untoward.'

'I see.'

'And, of course' (remembering that even as cynical an actor as Charles Paris had his professional pride) 'because you would be absolutely ideal for the part.'

Charles inclined his head graciously and looked up for more information.

'You see, Charles, the reason I thought of you was because of that business in Edinburgh that you sorted out . . . the murder of that boy—what was his name— Marinello?'

'Something like that. I'm flattered, Gerald, but I think to say I sorted it out is a slight exaggeration. I was there. . . .'

'It comes to the same thing. And then there was the Marius Steen business.'

'Again I would hardly say that I—'

'Don't worry what *you* think. I think you can do the job required and I'm asking you. I mean, it may be that there's nothing to investigate. In that case think of it just as an acting job. After the tour, you'd have a contract for nine months in the West End, you'd be pretty well paid—it's not a bad offer, is it?'

'No.'

'And you haven't got anything else major coming up at the moment, have you?'

As an actor, Charles replied instinctively, 'Well, there are one or two things I'm considering, which may possibly. . . .' Then he decided there was no point in trying to impress Gerald. 'No, nothing major.' Or why not be completely honest? 'Nothing minor either, as it happens. And I had a somewhat uncharitable letter from the Inland Revenue this morning.'

'So you'll take the job?'

'I suppose so.'

'That's terrific.' Gerald punctuated the agreement by refilling their wine glasses. He seemed relieved, which amazed Charles. Surely he never thought the offer might be refused. Or perhaps, from his position of extreme opulence, Gerald was unaware of the general scarcity of acting work at a time when theatres were paring down the size of their permanent companies, when big cast plays were no longer being written or produced and when even the BBC was making cutbacks in its programme hours. Nor was he probably aware of the precarious system of final demands and delaying letters by which Charles conducted his financial affairs.

'What about a sweet?' Gerald airily summoned the waiter with a well-tailored gesture and, as often before, Charles was impressed and amused by his friend's smoothness. He did not envy it, he had long ago decided that certain sorts of success did not interest him, but it was still entertaining to see a successful man at work. Everything about Gerald was right—the beautifully cut charcoal grey pin-striped suit, the residual tan from an August spent with his family in their villa in Corsica, the silver hair cut just long enough to be trendy, the chunky gold ring and identity bracelet, the almost imperceptible aura of expensive after-shave. Charles was always amazed by people who could live like figures in glossy magazines and by people who wanted to. For him the basic challenge of getting from day to day more than occupied his time.

The sweets were sorted out and they both tucked into monster slices of strawberry gâteau. Charles wiped a stray blob of cream from the side of his mouth and asked, 'What's been happening, Gerald?'

'In the show, you mean?'

'Yes. There must be something strange for you to go to these lengths to get me involved.'

'Yes. Two things have happened. They may both have been accidents, and they may be completely unconnected, but it's just possible that someone's trying to sabotage the whole venture.'

'What were the "accidents"?'

'The first came on the second day of rehearsal. There was a guy called Frederick Wooland who was rehearsal

pianist for the show. As he was on the way to the Welsh
Dragon Club where they're rehearsing, he was shot at.'

'Shot at? You mean someone tried to kill him?'

'No, not really. It was only an air rifle. He just got a
pellet in his hand. Not very serious except that he won't be
able to play for a couple of weeks and they've had to find a
new rehearsal pianist.'

'Usually if you hear of someone being shot at with an
air rifle, it's just kids fooling about.'

'Yes, I agree. That may well be what it was in this case.
It's a fairly rough area down there.'

'Where is the Welsh Dragon Club?'

'Elephant and Castle.'

'Hmm. Presumably the pianist didn't see who shot at
him?'

'No. First thing he knew was a stinging pain in his
hand.'

'Were the police told?'

'Oh yes. It was all official. They seemed to think it was
kids. No great surprise. It's not the first time that it's
happened round there.'

'In that case, I can't see why you think there's anything
odd about it. It doesn't sound as if it had anything to do
with the show at all. Perhaps the only lesson is that
managements should be prepared to pay a bit more
money to get rehearsal rooms in slightly nicer areas.' He
pronounced the last two words in his best Kensington
Lady accent.

'Okay. Yes, I admit, on its own, that doesn't sound
much. But exactly a week later there was another
accident. The day before yesterday.'

'What happened this time?'

'One of the actors fell down some stairs and broke his
leg.'

'Where? At the rehearsal rooms?'

'No. At his digs.'

'So why should that have anything to do with the
show?'

'It's just the coincidence of the two of them, exactly a

week apart, at exactly the same time of day, both people in the show.'

'What time of day was it?'

'Early in the morning both times. Frederick Wooland was shot on his way to rehearsal, say at quarter to ten, and Everard Austick was found in his digs at about half past nine this Tuesday.'

'Did you say Everard Austick?'

'Yes.'

Charles burst out laughing. 'You can't be serious.'

'What do you mean?'

'Well, Everard Austick is the greatest piss-artist in the business. He's a bottle-a-day man. Always drunk out of his mind. If you think that him having a fall in his digs is a sign of foul play, you're way off beam. I'd be much more suspicious if a day went by when he *didn't* fall down something.'

Gerald looked discomfited. 'Oh, I thought the coincidence was too great. I mean, both on the same day.'

'Well... it doesn't sound much to me. Listen, Gerald, I'm very grateful to you for getting me this job and certainly once I get inside the company I will investigate anything that needs investigating, but from what you've said, I'm not going to have much to do. Is that really all you've got?'

'Well, I suppose that's all the actual facts. But it means that the show has got off to an unlucky start and we—they don't want anything to go wrong. There's a lot of money at stake.'

'Whose money?'

Gerald didn't rise to the bait. 'Amulet Productions are putting up most of it and they're working in association with Arthur Balcombe, who is one of my clients. Hence my involvement.'

'I see. All the big boys.'

'Yes. And then of course Christopher Milton has a stake because he's got the rights of the show.'

'Christopher Milton?'

'Yes, he bought it as a vehicle for himself.'

'Really?'

'Didn't you know?'

'Gerald, you didn't tell me anything. You just asked if I would be prepared to take a part in a West End musical for nine months and keep my eyes open for any possible sabotage attempts. You've told me nothing about the show. But I see now, it's this musical based on *She Stoops to Conquer,* isn't it?'

'That's right.'

'I've seen stuff about it in the Press. Now let me think. . . .' he mused facetiously. 'If it's a musical based on *She Stoops to Conquer* for a West End audience, then what would it be called? Um. How about *Conkers?* With an exclamation mark.'

'No, it was going to be,' said Gerald with complete seriousness, 'but then it was decided that that didn't really give the right impression of the sort of show it is.'

'So what's it called now?'

'Lumpkin!'

'With an exclamation mark?'

'Of course.'

'With Christopher Milton as Tony Lumpkin?'

'Of course. That was another reason for the title. It means a neat billing—"Christopher Milton *as Lumpkin!*" See what I mean?'

'Yes, I do. Tony Lumpkin. Of course. One of the all-time great upstaging parts. Hmm. What's the script like?'

Gerald was reticent. 'It's okay.'

'Anything to do with Goldsmith?'

'No. He hasn't any money in it.'

'I didn't mean Goldsmith the impresario. I meant Oliver Goldsmith who wrote the thing.'

'Oh, I'm sorry. I think the show makes the occasional nod in his direction.'

'But presumably it's not designed for fans of Oliver Goldsmith?'

'No, it's designed for fans of Christopher Milton. He's riding very high at the moment, with the telly show at the top of the ratings.'

'What telly show?'

'Oh, come on, Charles, don't be affected. You must have seen *Straight Up, Guv*.'

'I don't think I have. I'm not a great telly viewer.' He did not possess a television in his Bayswater bed-sitter. He was not enthusiastic about the medium. It was a necessary evil for his career as an actor, because it was well paid, but he had never enjoyed the work (or the product).

'Well, let me enlighten your ignorance. The show gets massive audience figures and it has made Christopher Milton just about the hottest property around. He's very big box office.'

'So it doesn't really matter what show you put him in.'

'Ah, but it does, and *Lumpkin!* is just right. Could make a lot of money. That's way I—the people I represent—are so anxious that nothing should go wrong. Either to the show—or to the star.'

'I see. Who's written it?'

'Well, it's basically a show which the Ipswich Warehouse Company put on last year to celebrate the bicentenary of Goldsmith's death.'

'Oh yes, I remember reading a notice of that in *The Stage*. What was it called then?'

'*Liberty Hall*.'

'That's right.'

'Book by a chap called Kevin McMahon, with music by some bloke whose name I forget. Anyway, Christopher Milton's agent, Dickie Peck—do you know him, by the way?'

'By reputation.'

'Well, he went down and saw the show and reckoned it had potential for his boy, got Christopher Milton himself down to see it, and they bought up the rights. I think they got them pretty cheap. Could be a good investment. I mean, the stage show should run at least a couple of years on Christopher Milton's name, and then there might be a chance of a film. . . .'

'And the script is more or less as at Ipswich?'

'Hardly. No, there's been quite a lot of surgery. They've scrapped the original music and lyrics—or most of them anyway. And got in Carl Anthony and Micky Gorton to write new ones.'

'You look at me as if I should have heard of them.'

'You certainly should, Charles. They've written a whole string of Top Ten hits. *Heart Doctor ... Gimme No More Lies ... Disposable Man*—all that lot!'

'Ah.'

'Really, Charles, you are square.' Gerald prided himself on his sudden knowledge of the pop scene.

'Some of us age quicker than others, man.'

Gerald ignored the dig. 'The new music is excellent. It fits the style of the period, but it's also very ... funky.' He tried too hard to deliver the last word naturally.

Charles laughed. 'It sounds a riot. I hope I don't have to sing anything funky. I wouldn't know where to begin. Incidentally, I should have asked before—what part am I playing?'

'You're playing Sir Charles Marlow. Do you know the play?'

'Yes, I did a production of it once in Cardiff—with Bernard Walton of all people, when he was very new in the business. He played Young Marlow—his first starring rôle. And I'm the father ... hmm. Only comes in at the end.'

'That's right.'

'Good.'

'Why good?'

'Last act parts are good. You can spend the whole evening in the pub.'

'It was Everard Austick's part,' said Gerald reprovingly.

'Ah, yes, that was probably his downfall. A lifetime of last act parts is the short route to alcoholism.'

'Hmm.' Gerald pondered for a moment. 'I sometimes think I drink too much. Difficult to avoid in my line of work. Occupational hazard.'

'That's what I feel about my line of work too,' Charles agreed. 'Though I must admit at times I worry about the amount I put away.'

'Yes.' There was a reflective pause. Then Gerald said, 'How about a brandy?'

'Love one.'

When it arrived, Charles raised his glass. 'Many thanks, Gerald. This is the most painless audition I've ever undergone.'

'My pleasure.'

'Incidentally, I don't know anything about the time-scale on this show yet. What's this—the second week of rehearsal?'

'That's right. Second of five. Then the show does one week in Leeds....'

'Ah, Leeds....'

'Friends up there?'

'You could say that.'

'Then a week at Bristol, a week at Brighton, a week of final rehearsal and previews in town and then it should open at the King's Theatre on November 27th.'

'Isn't that a bit near Christmas? I mean, it's a dodgy time for audiences.'

Gerald smiled smugly. 'No problem. Christopher Milton's name will carry us over Christmas. And then...we'll be all right. Ideal family entertainment. Nothing to offend anyone.'

'I see. And when do I start rehearsal?'

'Tomorrow morning, if all goes well.'

'If all goes well? You mean, if I'm not poisoned overnight by the mysterious saboteur.'

'You may laugh, but I've a feeling there's something up.'

'I will keep my eyes skinned, word of honour.' Charles made a Boy Scout salute.

'And if you do find out anything...untoward or criminal, let me know first.'

'Before the police?'

'If possible. We have to watch the publicity angle on this.'

'I see.'

'We don't want the fuzz queering our pitch.'

Charles smiled. It was reassuring to hear Gerald dropping into his thriller slang. The solicitor had always had the sneaking suspicion that crime held more exciting dimensions than the minor infringements of contracts which occupied his working life. His thirst for criminal glamour had to be satisfied by thrillers and, in moments of excitement, his language showed it. Gerald was excited now. He thought they were on to a case.

Charles didn't. He felt certain that the whole idea of saboteurs had been dreamt up by nervy managements suddenly counting up the amount of money that they had invested in one stage show and one star. They were scared and they had to give what frightened them a tangible form. Sabotage was as good an all-purpose threat as any other.

Still, he wasn't complaining. Nine months' work, however boring it might be, was nine months' work. It could sort out the taxman and one or two other pressing problems.

'I'll be very discreet, Gerald, and tell you everything.'

'Good.'

'Now let me buy you a brandy.'

'I wouldn't worry. It's all on Arthur Balcombe. You didn't really think I was taking you out on my own money?'

'No, Gerald, I know you never do anything on your own money. Still, let's have another brandy on Arthur Balcombe and imagine that I've bought it to thank you for the job.'

'Okay. There is one thing, though.'

'Yes.'

'I've offered you the job, you've accepted it, but in a way it isn't mine to offer.'

'Now he tells me.'

'I mean, I don't think there'll be any problem, but it's just that you'll have to go and see Dickie Peck before it's all definite.'

'Oh.'

'Just to check details of your contract.'

'*Just* to check details of my contract.'

'Well, it's also . . . sort of . . . to get to know you, to see if you are the kind of person who's likely to get on with Christopher Milton, if you see what I—'

'What you mean by that formula of words is that Christopher Milton has an Approval of Cast clause in his contract and I've got to go and see Dickie Peck to be vetted.'

Gerald tried to find another formula of words, but eventually was forced to admit that that was exactly what he meant.

'I get it. When do I see Peck?'

'You've got an appointment at four o'clock.'

Two...

DICKIE PECK WORKED for Creative Artists Ltd, one of the biggest film and theatre agencies in the country, and he was big. His clients were said to be managed by 'Dickie Peck at Creative Artists' rather than just by 'Creative Artists'. In the agency world this designation often preceded a split from the parent company when an individual member of the staff would set up on his own (usually taking his best clients with him). But Dickie Peck had had this individual billing ever since anyone could remember and showed no signs of leaving the Creative Artists umbrella. There was no point in his making the break; he was a director of the company and worked within it in his own way at his own pace.

It was the pace which was annoying Charles as he sat waiting in the Creative Artists Reception in Bond Street. He had been informed by the over-made-up girl on the switchboard that Mr Peck was not yet back from lunch and as the clock ticked round to half past four, Charles felt all the resentment of someone who has finished lunch at half past three.

He was not alone in Reception. A young actress with carefully highlighted cheek-bones was reading *The Stage* and sighing dramatically from time to time; an actor whose old, hollow eyes betrayed his startlingly golden hair gave a performance of nonchalance by staring at his buckled patent leather shoes. The girl on the switchboard kept up a low monologue of 'A call for you . . .', 'I'm sorry, he's tied up at the moment...' and 'Would you mind hanging on?' She deftly snapped plugs in and out like a weaver at her loom.

It was nearly a quarter to five when Dickie Peck came through Reception. The girl on the switchboard stage-whispered, 'Mr Peck, there've been a couple of calls and there's a gentleman waiting to see you.'

He half-turned and Charles got an impression of a cigar with a long column of ash defying gravity at its end. Ignoring his visitor, the agent disappeared into his office. Five minutes later a summons came through on the receptionist's intercom.

The office was high over Bond Street and Dickie Peck's chair backed on to a bow-window. Cupboards and dusty glass-fronted book-cases lined the walls. The paint-work must once have been cream, but had yellowed with age. The dark red carpet smelt of dust. Nothing much on the desk. A current *Spotlight*, Actors LZ (to check what Charles Paris looked like) and a circular ash-tray in the centre of which was a decorative half golf-ball. The channel around this was full of lengths of cigar ash, long and obscene, like turds.

The ash was long on the cigar that still drooped from the agent's lips. It was an expensive one, but the end was so chewed and worried that it looked like the cheap brown-wrapping-paper sort.

The face which the cigar dwarfed was grey and lined, crowned by a long tongue of hair brushed inadequately over baldness. The head was disproportionately small and accentuated the stocky bulk of body below it. Dickie Peck was dressed in a dark grey suit with thin lapels. A plain blue tie askew across a grubby white shirt. Tie and jacket dusted with cigar ash. It was not the traditional image of the big show business agent; more like a Town Hall clerk.

'Charles Paris, isn't it? Take a chair.' He gestured expansively, but the ash at the end of his cigar miraculously stayed intact.

Charles sat on a low gilt chair whose red plush upholstery was as hard as wood.

'Now, Mr Paris, I gather you've seen a representative of Amulet Productions about this part.'

'Yes.' So Gerald wasn't just acting as solicitor for Arthur Balcombe.

'And he explained what it was about?'

'Yes.'

'Good. As you gather, the part became vacant due to an accident to one of the cast.'

'I know.' Charles didn't volunteer any comment. Gerald had been uncertain whether Dickie Peck shared his suspicions of sabotage or not and had asked Charles to play it carefully. The fewer people knew that there was an investigator in the company, the better.

Dickie Peck gave no sign of suspicion. He took a long draw at his cigar, extending the column of ash to an even more precarious length. He leant back and blew a slow jet of smoke to the ceiling. 'This show, Mr Paris, is a very big one.'

'So I gather.' Charles was getting tired of being told about the size of the operation.

'It's likely to be a very big success.'

'Good,' said Charles, feeling that some sort of comment was required.

'And so it's important that everything about it should be right.'

Again Charles helped out the pause with a 'Yes'.

'Because what we have here is a show with a very big star. Christopher Milton, no less.'

Here a longer pause was left for some comment of amazed approbation. Charles produced a grunt which he hoped was appropriate.

'Yes, Christopher Milton. Let me tell you, Mr Paris, I have been in this business a very long time and I have never before seen someone who had so much star quality written all over him.'

'Ah.' Charles found it difficult to get interested in the idea of stardom. It was not the end of show business in which he was involved.

But Dickie Peck's litany had started and couldn't be stopped. 'Oh yes, I've seen them all sitting in that chair.

They've all come to me for advice. Because they know, if they want to get ahead in this business, then they should come and see old Dickie Peck. Oh yes.' For the first time in the interview he looked at the crumbling end of his cigar, but decided it didn't need attention yet. 'I remember once back in 1960, I had four young men from Liverpool in this office. Four ordinary lads, got their own group—would I be interested in representing them? And you know who they were? Only the Beatles.

'They asked my advice and I gave it. I said, Lads, you've got a lot of talent, but the act isn't right. What you've got to do is split up, go your own ways, separate careers, that's what you need if you're really going to make it.' He paused for dramatic emphasis, then delivered his triumph. 'And look at them now—separate careers.'

He leant back with satisfaction, then, instinctively sensing the imminent collapse of his cigar ash, deposited another neat cylinder into the ash-tray.

'There have been others too—Frank Sinatra once when he was over here, wanted a bit of advice on which way I thought his career should go. Glenda Jackson, Tom Jones, oh yes, they've all sat in that chair and asked for a bit of help from old Dickie Peck.'

Charles looked at the chair on which he was sitting with what he hoped was due reverence and didn't believe a word of it.

'But let me tell you, Mr Paris, of all the big stars I've ever seen, Christopher Milton is the biggest. That boy has so much talent, he can do anything. I mean, when you think that he is now only thirty-four, a mere baby, at the beginning of his career, I tell you in the future there's going to be no stopping him. And *Lumpkin!* is the show that's really going to put him in the big time.' Realising that this could be constructed as diminishing his protégé, he covered himself. 'Not of course that he isn't in the big time already. With the television show, a few films, oh yes, he's right at the top. And it's not that we haven't had offers—oh, there have been plenty of scripts come along, plenty of managements with ideas, chance of a big musical on Broadway, Hollywood positively begging, but we said no. We preferred to bide our time, wait for the right show, the one that was absolutely right. Christopher Milton had got the telly, he was doing okay, he could affort to wait. That's an important thing in this business, choosing the right work. Oh yes, you've got to be selective.'

Which is nice if you can afford to be selective, thought Charles. Most actors have to do what comes along or starve.

Dickie Peck's monologue was evidently self-propelled, so Charles gave up providing nods and yesses and grunts of agreement to stimulate it. 'Now, of course, when you're talking about an artist of Christopher Milton's calibre, you want to be sure that all the work he does is done in the right atmosphere, that he works with people who he gets on with, people who are sympathetic to what he's doing.' Charles pricked up his ears. They were finally getting round to the vetting part of the interview. 'Because what happens when you get someone with more talent than most people is that you do tend to get jealousy developing. And that doesn't make for a healthy working atmosphere in a company. Now Christopher Milton is a charming boy, very easy to get along with, but he is a person of considerable genius and he does have strong ideas. Now because of his great sense of theatre his ideas are very often right. And obviously in the context of a show being rehearsed under pressure, too many arguments over the way things are done can only be counter-productive. Do you see what I mean?'

He leant back, nursing another two inches of cigar ash. This time a response was definitely needed.

And it was not an easy one to give. Oh yes, Charles knew what Dickie Peck meant. Through all the verbiage, the message was quite clear—if you want this job, you will have to undertake to do as Christopher Milton says. He's not the director of the show, but his word is law, and if you don't like the sound of that, remember he has an Approval of Casting clause and the world is full of unemployed actors.

Under normal circumstances Charles liked to think

he'd tell the agent to stuff his job and walk out. But these weren't normal circumstances. He tried to conciliate his conscience. Gerald had offered him the job, and Gerald was a friend. It wouldn't do to let him down. Anyway, it wasn't really an acting job. He was being infiltrated into the company as an investigator of sabotage. Yes, it was quite legitimate for him to accept the conditions; it would only raise suspicion if he didn't. But as he replied, he knew that his real motive was the tax bill lying on the table in his room in Hereford Road. 'Yes, I fully understand, Mr Peck. I know that Christopher Milton owns the rights of the show and so obviously he will be deeply concerned in all aspects of the production, and I'm sure I will respect his ideas.'

Dickie Peck looked at him suspiciously, but evidently decided to take the reply at face value. 'Good, fine. Well, we have Mr Venables' word as to your suitability for the part. . . .' Then, just as Gerald had done, he gave a token nod to actor's pride. 'And of course I know your work. I have a script of the show here. Did Mr Venables tell you about the tour and the length of contract?'

'Yes.'

'Fine. Well, good luck.'

'Thank you. There is just one thing. . . .'

'Oh, yes, of course, money.'

'Yes. Look, I'll give you my agent's number. He deals with all that.'

'Fine. Will I catch him there now? I'd like to get this sorted out today. And it's after half past five now.'

'Maurice'll be there. He works from home anyway.'

'Fine. I'll give him a buzz.'

'Well, thank you very much, Mr Peck. I hope that show's going to be a great success.'

'With Christopher Milton in it it's bound to be. That boy is what stardom's all about. Oh yes, it'll be a big success. And if anyone tries to stop it being a success, there'll be hell to pay. Christopher Milton is going right to the top and no one is going to get in his way.'

He said the last words with a fierce, almost religious, intensity.

Charles pressed twopence into the coin-box when he heard the voice say, 'Maurice Skellern Artistes'.

'Maurice.'

'Who's calling him?'

'Oh, for God's sake, Maurice, don't you ever recognise my voice? It's me—Charles.'

'Ah well, can't be too careful in this business. Don't want to give anything away.'

'You don't give much away by answering to your name. Anyway, never mind that. Did Dickie Peck get through to you?'

'Yes, Charles. Sounds very good, this musical. I think it's about time you got into that sort of show. I mean, haven't I been saying for years that you ought to be doing shows that are more...more important?'

'No. You've been saying for years that I ought to be doing shows that are better paid.'

'Ah, now that's not fair, Charles. Okay, I've always said you should keep out of these fringe capers, this experimental stuff, but I've always been thinking primarily of your career, of your artistic development.'

'That's very generous of you.'

'I do my best.'

'So what am I getting for the current artistic development?'

'Well, Charles, Dickie Peck was offering, on behalf of the management, twenty-five for rehearsal, forty on tour and sixty for the run and I said you wouldn't consider it for under forty for rehearsal, eighty on tour and a hundred for the run and I wouldn't budge from that and that was my final word on the subject.'

'So?'

'You're getting thirty for rehearsal, fifty on tour and eighty for the run.'

'Oh well, could be worse. Christopher Milton's in this show. Got any form on him?' While Maurice Skellern was pretty useless as an agent, he was an invaluable source of theatrical gossip.

'Nothing much, no. He doesn't do a lot of work, really.'

'It's just that everything he does is massively successful.'

'Yes, if you look back on his career it's all award-winning shows. Not a lot, but it's all been chosen just right.'

'That's what having a good agent is about.'

Maurice didn't seem to notice the edge in the remark. 'He's a talented boy, Charles.'

'Where did he start?'

'I'm fairly sure he came out of one of the stage schools, but I don't know which one. Think he may have been a child star in films. Not sure, though.'

'Know anything of his working reputation?'

'A bit temperamental, I've heard. But that's third hand. I mean stories like that go around about every big name in the business.'

'Yes. Is he gay or anything?'

'No, I don't think so. Sure not, actually. He married that girl who was in that film . . . you know.'

'I'm afraid I don't.'

'Oh, the one who played opposite Nigel Thingummy in that. . . . Oh, you know. Name like Elsa or Virginia or—Charlotte Fable, that's it!'

'I've heard of her. Still together?'

'No, I think they split up eighteen months or so ago.'

'Divorce?'

'Haven't seen anything about it. No, I shouldn't think he'd like the publicity. Rather lets down the image of lovability, and that's what the public expects of him.'

'Hmm. Oh well, thanks.'

'If you really want form, ask Johnny Wilson. He worked with him on the telly show.'

'Oh yes. What's that called?'

'*Straight Up, Guv.* Surely you must have seen it.'

'No, I haven't.'

'Oh, it's a very funny show, Charles. I never miss it. It's on tonight at seven-thirty. These are repeats, actually, second time round, or is it third? Think of the money on a show like that. Probably sells round the world. That's what you need, Charles, a big, long-running television series.'

'As part of my artistic development?'
'Of course.'

That evening Charles watched television. He went round
to see Jim Waldeman, a fellow actor who lived in Queen's
Gardens with his wife Susie and a fairly new baby. He
took a bottle of Bell's to ensure his welcome, but it was
unnecessary. As he entered the door, both Jim and Susie's
eyes lit up and, with a cry of 'Baby-sitter!', they installed
him in an arm-chair in front of the television and went off
to the pictures. 'Imagine,' said Susie, 'actually going to see
a film. The excitement. We used to go about twice a week,
but since *that* came along, we just haven't. At all. Bless
you, Charles.'

'What happens if it—'

'Oh, he won't. He's terribly good. But if he does, there's
some Phenergan on the dresser. Cheerio.' And the door
slammed.

'What's Phenergan?' asked Charles weakly, but he
realised they couldn't hear. He also realised that the slam
of the door had woken the baby.

He switched on the television, determined that the
child would soon be asleep again. It was a colour set
(Jim's career was obviously flourishing), but Charles
caught the end of an old black and white movie. It was
British, some story about a small boy bringing together
his estranged parents. The father was an airman and there
was a lot of stiff upper lip stuff about one last mission. The
boy was a beautiful child, with a perfectly proportioned
baby face and blond curls. Charles wondered idly if it was
Christopher Milton in his child star days.

It was becoming clear that the baby was not going back
to sleep. The keening cry sawed through the noise of the
television. Charles looked at his watch. Twenty-five past
seven. The crying showed no signs of abating and he
didn't want to miss the beginning of the show. He went
into the night-lit nursery and mumbled soothingly over
the cot. The screams redoubled in volume. In the
sitting-room music built to an heroic conclusion. He
picked up the baby in its blanket and returned to the
television.

The film credits flashed past. The child star was not Christopher Milton. Gareth Somebody, another who had no doubt vanished without trace to become an accountant or an estate agent or a double glazing salesman. After the film came a trailer for a programme on Northern Ireland to be shown the following night.

The baby was not taking kindly to its move. The little mouth strained open like a goldfish and the pebble eyes almost vanished in folds of skin as it screamed. It was a long time since Charles had held a baby and he had forgotten the little tricks he had used when his own daughter Juliet was small. He tried rocking the little bundle and murmuring the Skye Boat Song. It didn't work.

On the television screen the credits rolled. Inevitably, 'CHRISTOPHER MILTON' came first. Then 'in STRAIGHT UP, GUV—by WALLY WILSON'. Then 'with' the names of a couple of those comedy supports who are never out of work and the inevitable wild studio applause faded into the show proper. (Why do studio audiences always applaud signature tunes and credits? The fact that they clap when nothing has happened casts serious doubts on the credibility of their subsequent reactions.) The episode started; Charles couldn't hear a word above the baby's howls.

In desperation he dipped a finger in his Scotch and proffered it to the bellowing mouth. The tiny lips closed round it as if determined to remove the skin. But there was silence.

It didn't last. After a few moments the suction was released and the bellowing recommenced. Charles hastily dipped his finger back in the glass and the mouth clamped on again. By repeating the process every two minutes he found he could watch *Straight Up, Guv* in comparative comfort.

It was not bad. The show was built around the adventures of a second-rate con-man Lionel Wilkins (played of course by Christopher Milton), whose attempts to pull off the big coup were always crowned with disaster. Wally Wilson's script was workmanlike, but uninspired; it was Christopher Milton's performance which raised it above the ordinary. Lionel Wilkins was a genuine comic creation, whose doomed cockiness was strangely engaging. He was the original Wobbly Man; every time you pushed him over, he bounced back up again. As catastrophe followed catastrophe and his face crumpled into crestfallen embarrassment, the audience roared. Each time he picked himself up with some new incongruous scheme and the audience roared again. Even Charles found himself laughing out loud at times. Christopher Milton's face in repose was unremarkable, but in the character it seemed capable of infinite comic variation. It was easy to see why the show had become a cult.

And, like many cult shows, it had a catch-phrase. As the worst reversal hit him, Lionel Wilkins paused in horror, the audience laughed in anticipation, and then, with perfect timing, he said, 'I beg yours?' As Charles heard it, he recognised it, recognised it from shouting schoolboys in the street, giggling secretaries in the tube and half-heard impressionists on the radio. 'I beg yours?' was Christopher Milton; he said it and the entire nation followed him.

When Jim and Susie returned, Charles and the baby were still watching television, and between them they'd got through half the bottle of Bell's.

Three...

THE WELSH DRAGON Club near the Elephant and Castle
had been built in more elegant times as a meeting-place
for expatriate Welshmen of the upper and middle classes.
It then boasted four tennis courts (grass), fielded six
rugby teams and held very proper dances on Saturdays.
The members tended to wear blazers or tweed, they had
strong religious principles and, when drunk, broke into
mournful song.

The club was now lost in a forest of concrete blocks.
Two of the tennis courts had been sold for development
and the others were now pink shale stained with moss.
The only rugby discussed in the bar was what was seen on
the television and the Saturday dances had been replaced
by intermittent bookings for disco-parties (which were
rarely profitable because of the number of broken
windows). The members had gone down in class and
numbers. They tended to lounge around in jeans and
patterned pullovers, propped against the moth-eaten
baize of the old notice-boards, occasionally throwing a
desultory dart or pulling without hope at the arm of the
one fruit machine. When they got drunk, they still broke
into mournful song.

The club had one paid employee, who doubled the
rôles of caretaker and barman. His name was Griff and he
spent whole days propped over the bar reading an
apparently inexhaustible copy of the *Sun*.

The club activities could not possibly make any profit,

but the Welsh Dragon stayed open. All its revenue came
from hiring out rehearsal rooms. There were two—one
where old cue-racks and brass score-boards against
treacle-coloured panels accentuated the absence of the
long-sold billiard tables, and the other, grandly called the
'Ballroom', a long expanse of bare boards with a tiny
stage at one end and a wall of French windows which in
the old days were left open for dances after summer
tournaments. Many of the window panes had been
broken and covered with asymmetrical offcuts of
hardboard.

Charles was directed to the Ballroom, where a flotsam
of chairs and upturned benches represented the expensive
set of *Lumpkin!* (The designs, by Derbyshire Wilkes, were
elaborate and featured considerable use of revolves and
flown pieces.) The scene was like any morning in any
rehearsal room. Actors and actresses sat on chairs round
the edges of the room like the sad wallflowers who had
once moped there after missing vital backhand returns in
the mixed doubles. Little clusters formed round
crosswords or gossip. Bleary bodies shuffled slowly out of
the cocoons of their coats. A member of the stage
management moved purposefully around the room,
following some logic of her own. Hangovers and
television were discussed, knitting was unwound.

The director, David Meldrum, was poring over the
script at a small table isolated in the middle of the room.
He was balding, with rimless glasses and somehow
managed the pinched look of a clerk from a Dickens
serial. Charles knew him by sight and introduced himself.

'Ah, Charles, hello. I gathered your name was being
mentioned for the part. Nice to see you.' He did not seem
particularly interested in the addition to his cast.
'Gwyneth will give you a rehearsal schedule.'

At the mention of her name, the stage management girl
homed in and handed Charles a cyclostyled sheet of times
and scenes. Instinctively he assessed her. Old habits die
hard and one of the first moves on joining any company is
to examine the available crumpet. He decided that

Gwyneth looked too dauntingly efficient for his taste. Not a high cuddlability rating.

As he sat down to study the schedule, Charles reflected that it was rather pathetic for him still to be studying the crumpet. He was nearly forty-nine years old and his emotional track record was not spectacular. There was a nice wife, Frances, in Muswell Hill, with whom he hadn't lived for fourteen years (in spite of occasional reconciliations) and who was now reputed to have a boy friend. Apart from her, it was a history of intense casual affairs, which were either too intense or too casual. Thinking about it depressed him, so he channelled his thoughts in another direction.

It was strange that David Meldrum had accepted his appearance so casually. Indeed, it was strange that the director had had no part in his selection for the rôle. 'I gathered your name was being mentioned for the part.' As if it had nothing to do with him. Charles racked his brains for any stray comments he had heard about the director and from some source he couldn't identify he remembered the words, 'A good technician, love, but about as much imagination as a bread-board. Ought really to be in local government. Approaches a production like planning a car park.' That made sense. David Meldrum was a director who would see that the show got on the stage. He might not have many ideas of his own, but at least he wouldn't argue with anyone else's. Charles felt certain that Christopher Milton's contract also included an Approval of Director clause.

He looked round for the star, but there was no sign of him. Five to ten. Perhaps he was one of those actors who makes a point of arriving just at the moment of the call.

As the room filled up, there were one or two familiar faces from a long time ago. He saw Michael Peyton, with whom he'd worked on his own production of *She Stoops to Conquer* in Cardiff. They grinned at each other across the room. A couple of other actors smiled vaguely, as unable to remember Charles' name as he was to remember theirs.

There were few actresses. Thinking of the original play, Charles could only remember three female characters— Mrs Hardcastle, Kate Hardcastle and Miss Neville. He identified them easily. The middle-aged lady in a tweed trouser-suit and a scallop of blue-grey hair he recognised as Winifred Tuke. Good workmanlike actress. He remembered once overhearing her saying, 'Been a feature player all my life and very happy at it—I've never wanted to be a star.' She must be playing Mrs Hardcastle. The thin girl with aquiline nose and straight blonde hair must be Miss Neville and the shorter one whose mouth and teeth were attractively too large looked absolutely right for Kate Hardcastle.

Michael Peyton came over to chat and confirmed the identification. The girl playing Kate was called Lizzie Dark, apparently only a year out of Sussex University and generally believed to have a glowing future.

'Nice looking kid, isn't she?' Charles observed.

'Yes. Fairly regular boy friend. Often comes and picks her up after rehearsals.'

'Oh, I wasn't thinking. . . .'

'Of course you were.'

'Well. . . .'

'There's always the tour.'

'Hmm.'

'And the dancers.'

'When do they join us?'

'Next week. They're rehearsing separately.'

'How the hell do dancers fit into *She Stoops to Conquer?*'

'If you think this show bears any relation to the play as we did it in Cardiff, you can't have read the script.'

'True. I've only read my scenes.'

'There's an actor for you. I hope you didn't count your lines.'

'No,' he lied.

David Meldrum stood up and moved to the centre of the set in a rather apologetic way. 'Um, perhaps we ought to start. . . .'

He was interrupted by the entry of a man in a

donkey-jacket, who whispered something to him and sat
down on a chair adjacent to the table. He had brown curly
hair and a boyish face with a snub nose, but his skin belied
the impression of youth. It had that *papier-mâché*e
quality which is the legacy of bad acne.

'Who's he?' Charles hissed.

'Spike. He's the stage manager. Nice bloke. He must be
down to see if we're actually going to be able to negotiate
Derbyshire Wilkes' amazing set. Of course, there's always
the stage staff,' he added irrelevantly.

'What do you mean?'

'Potential crumpet.'

'I'm too old.'

'Come off it. Nothing like a warm little props girl to
comfort a chap in his old age.'

'Um, I think we should make a start,' said David
Meldrum.

'Where's the star, Michael?'

'Oh, he's never called till ten-thirty. It's in his contract.'

In 1773 Oliver Goldsmith decided that Sir Charles
Marlow should not appear in his play until the fifth act, so
Charles Paris' rehearsal schedule was not too onerous.
That much had survived the translation of *She Stoops to
Conquer* into *Liberty Hall* and even the transmogrifica-
tion of *Liberty Hall* into *Lumpkin!* The result was that,
although there was ground to be made up and Charles
would have to go through his scenes with the assistant
director and be taxied off to Soho for a costume fitting
that afternoon, he was not actually called for the
morning. And because Griff the barman interpreted such
concepts as club membership and licensing hours with a
commendable degree of independence, by ten-thirty
Charles and Michael Peyton were sitting in the bar over a
couple of pints of bitter.

Griff was hunched over the *Sun*, reading between the
lines of a photograph. In the corner a gloomy figure in
denim battledress confronted the fruit machine, willing it
to swallow his money and confirm his failure. Charles
decided it might be a good moment to find if Gerald's

suspicions about the two accidents were shared by an ordinary member of the company like Michael Peyton. 'Funny way of coming into a show for me, you know, Mike. After an accident. Sort of dead men's shoes situation.'

'Ah well, it's an ill wind.'

'Yes. Poor old Everard.'

'No one can expect to drink that much and stay perpendicular. Against the laws of physics.'

'Yes. I suppose he just fell....'

'Suppose so,' said Michael without interest and certainly without suspicion.

'Hm.' No harm in probing a bit further. 'Funny, though, that accident coming straight after the other one.'

'Other one?'

'The rehearsal pianist.'

'Who? Alec?'

'No, the one before him.'

Michael jutted forward his lower lip in an expression of ignorance. 'Didn't know there was one.'

'Oh, I heard some rumour. Must have got it wrong.' Obviously to the ordinary member of the company there was nothing bizarre going on. There was no general feeling of doom, of a 'bad luck' show. Gerald's imagination had been overstimulated by thoughts of the size of his financial investment. For Charles, it was just an acting job. He raised his glass to his lips and reflected on the differences between unemployed drinking and drinking with a nine-month contract. A warm glow filled him.

'Griff love, can you do me a port.' The new voice belonged to a good-looking young man in a smart blazer and check trousers. 'I've got the most frightful throat coming on and David's just sent me to go through my songs with Alec up in the billiard room.'

'Port, eh?'

'It's the only thing for a throat, Griff.'

'Huh.'

'Mark, have you met Charles Paris?'

'No, Mike, I haven't. Hello, I'm Mark Spelthorne.' He

left an infinitesimal pause for Charles to say, 'Yes, of course, I recognise your face from the television,' but Charles didn't, so he continued. 'You're taking over from poor old Everard?'

'That's right.'

'Well, don't drink too much of that, or you'll go the same way.'

'I'll be careful.' It wasn't worth objecting to the young man's patronising tone.

'Do you know, Mike,' said Mark Spelthorne, though he was addressing the world in general rather than anyone in particular, 'my agent is a bloody fool. He had a call yesterday from Yorath Knightley—do you know him?'

'No.'

'BBC. Telly. Drama. Wanted me for a play, super part. Rehearsals the week after this opens. Lovely, just what I need. But my damn fool agent says, oh no, out of the question, they may have some rerehearsal and what have you on *Lumpkin!* Honestly. I said, well, surely, love, we can get a few days off, sort round the contract, organise the filming round the schedule for this show. Oh no, he says, you're under contract. No bloody imagination. I think I must get another agent.'

'Sorry it took so long. Had to open a bottle. Don't get much call for port here. One or two of the ladies has it with lemon, but most of the gents drink beer or spirits.'

'Never mind, Griff. Bless you,' said Mark Spelthorne bountifully. He took a sip of the drink and gargled it gently, then swallowed. 'Better.' He repeated the process. Charles and Mike watched in silence as the glass slowly emptied. 'Ah, well, better test out the old singing voice.'

'If you want to hear real singing,' said Griff morosely, 'you want to listen to a Welsh male voice choir.'

'Ah.' Mark was nonplussed, not certain what his reaction should be.

'We used to have a choir here at the Welsh Dragon. Lovely singing. Better than anything I've heard since you lot've been here.'

'That's a matter of opinion.' Mark hesitated, uncertain

whether or not that was a good enough exit line. Failing to come up with a better one, he exited to the billiard room.

'Should I know him, Mike? He behaved as if I should.'

'Not unless you're a fan of *The Fighter Pilots*, Charles.'

'What's that?'

'You're obviously not. It's an ITV series. Another cashing in on the nostalgia boom. Mark Spelthorne plays Flying Officer Falconer, whose daring missions and dreary love life fill up most of each episode.'

'Oh. I've never heard of him in the theatre.'

'I don't think he's done much. Presumably he did his forty weeks round the provinces to get the Equity card, but I think that's it. He's one of the media mushrooms who has sprung up overnight as a fully developed television star.'

'Then why is he in this?'

'Publicity, Charles. So that he can be billed on the poster as Mark Spelthorne of *The Fighter Pilots*. That's to mop up the one per cent of the population who haven't come to see Christopher Milton of *Straight Up, Guv*.'

'The television take-over is complete.'

'Yes.'

'He seemed to have a fairly inflated opinion of himself.'

'Ah, he would like to be a big star, Charles.'

'And will he make it?'

'I don't know. Somehow I don't think so. Don't think he's got what it takes.'

'What's he playing?'

'Your son, Young Marlow.'

'That's the best part in the play.'

'Was, Charles, was. Maybe that's what Goldsmith intended, but that was before Christopher Milton got his hands on the script.'

'Yes,' the gloomy man at the fruit machine chipped in suddenly and savagely. 'Before Christopher Milton got his bloody hands on the script.'

There was a moment's pause before Michael Peyton recovered himself sufficiently to make the introduction. 'Charles Paris—Kevin McMahon.'

'Ah yes. You wrote *Liberty Hall*.'

'In a previous existence, I think.' His voice had the rough blur of a hangover and there was a large Scotch on a table beside the fruit machine. Having registered his protest, he seemed to lose interest in the two actors and, with an air of self-mortification, pressed another ten pence into the slot. Or maybe he turned away as a deliberate snub to the man entering the bar. 'Morning, everyone. Hello, Griff. Charles Paris, isn't it?'

'That's right.'

'Delighted you're with us on the show.'

Charles took the offered firm handshake and looked into the clear, honest face. 'My name's Christopher Milton.'

Four...

THE NEXT FEW weeks were an education for Charles. The sort of theatre he had always concentrated on had not depended on stars. Christopher Milton was a star.

At their initial meeting he was charming. There was only a short break in rehearsal, but he devoted it all to the new member of the company. And he had done his homework. He referred to incidents in Charles' career which he could not have guessed at, but which showed genuine interest or research. He spoke flatteringly about the one successful play Charles had written, *The Ratepayer*. In fact all the right things were said and Charles was impressed. He saw once again the distorting mirror of show-biz rumour at work. Reputations get inflated and diminished by gossip and scandal. One bitchy remark by a jealous actor can give the permanent stigma of being 'difficult' to another. Time and again Charles had encountered supposedly 'lovely' people who were absolute monsters and been charmed by supposed monsters. And he found Christopher Milton charming.

As rehearsals developed and he began to feel part of the company, it was increasingly difficult to take Gerald's fears of sabotage seriously. There was an air of tension about the production, but no more than one would expect from any show at that stage of development. Charles' rôle was not an onerous one, and Griff's ever-open bar was an ideal place to toast Gerald's excessive anxiety which had got him the job.

He had a slight twinge of misgiving as the Tuesday approached. Gerald had made such an issue of the fact that the two accidents had taken place exactly a week apart. If there were a psychopathic wrecker about, determined to ruin the show, then he would strike again on the Tuesday.

Charles went to rehearsal that morning with some trepidation but the day passed and there wasn't so much as a cold among the cast. He decided that he had just landed on his feet in an acting job. Eighty pounds a week and sucks to the taxman.

*   *   *

He had not seen much of the show except for the scenes which involved him, but on the Wednesday he decided to stay on after he'd finished. They were rehearsing the Chase Scene at the end.

Now Goldsmith did not write a Chase Scene. In his play Tony Lumpkin meets Hastings and describes how he has just led Mrs Hardcastle and Miss Neville on a circular wild goose chase until, 'with a circumbendibus, I fairly lodged them in the horse-pond at the bottom of the garden'. But description is not the stuff of West End musicals. Kevin McMahon had written a small chase into *Liberty Hall* and had been persuaded to expand it for *Lumpkin!* The result was a massive production number with song and dance, as Tony Lumpkin actually led the two ladies in their coach through mire and thicket. The dancers, playing a series of misdirecting yokels, buxom country wenches and a full-scale fox hunt which would have amazed Goldsmith, were rehearsing elsewhere on their own, and the special effects of fog, rain and snow were not yet available. Nor was it possible to simulate the moving trees and revolving cottages which were to add visual excitement to the scene. But it was already a complicated sequence and an interesting one to watch.

It also gave Charles his first opportunity to see Christopher Milton in action, building a part. The result was impressive. Tony Lumpkin was emerging as a complete comic character, totally different from Lionel Wilkins. The London whine of the television con-man had been replaced by a rich West Country accent and instead of sentimental incompetence, there was a roguishly knowing confidence. Charles began to feel that Dickie Peck's claims for his client's talent were not so ridiculous.

David Meldrum had by now been nicknamed David Humdrum and it fitted. He ordered people round the acting space like a suburban gardener laying a patio. Everything had to be exactly in place, every move exactly matching the neat plans in his script. But it was not the perfectionism of genius; it was the predictability of a man who had worked out his blocking with pins on a stage model long before rehearsals had started.

Still, it was professional and efficient. The production advanced. And for a complex commercial show it's probably better to have a good journeyman than a genius.

Anyway, David Meldrum was only providing the skeleton; the flesh was the performances. And Christopher Milton was fleshing up nicely. He had a song called *Lead 'em Astray*, for which Micky Gorton had written some most ungoldsmithian lyrics.

> *'Get them going*
> *The wrong way*
> *There's no knowing*
> *What they'll say.*
> *Hey, hey, hey,*
> *Lead 'em astray.'*

If Gorton's lyrics did have a fault it was a tendency to the non-specific. They had been written not to advance the plot, but to be taken out of the show and recorded by pop stars. However, Carl Anthony's tunes were good and *Lead 'em Astray*, in spite of its anachronism, captured the excitement and mischief of Tony Lumpkin. In Christopher Milton's performance, even with just the rehearsal piano, it was a potential show-stopper.

It was also very funny. His movements were beautiful.

They showed the clodhopping clumsiness of the character and yet they were very precise. He darted round the two chairs which represented Mrs Hardcastle's coach and wove his way through the other chairs which were trees. On the chorus of the song he froze for a moment, then jerked forward like a car left in gear, then stopped and flashed a look of sheer devilment at the audience. The timing made the gesture hilarious; even the cast who had seen it many times before laughed spontaneously. He seemed encouraged by the reaction and in the next verse his movements became more grotesque and jerky. He bounced up to the coach and pecked forward like a chicken with a head that suddenly seemed disconnected from his body. There was a splutter from Miss Neville, the unmistakable sound of someone 'corpsing'. Christopher Milton rose to it and varied the steps of his dance into a strange little jig. This struck Miss Neville as even funnier and soon she was gaping, incapable with laughter, while tears flowed down her cheeks.

The laughter spread. Mrs Hardcastle started, then one by one, the watching actors caught it. Charles found himself giggling uncontrollably. It was one of those moments of communal hysteria which cannot be explained, but where everything suddenly gets funnier and funnier.

Only Christopher Milton stayed in control. The pianist was laughing too much to continue playing, but the star sang and danced on to the end of the number. His movements got faster and stranger and funnier until suddenly at the end he dropped flat on his back.

The timing was immaculate. It was the perfect end to the sequence. And it was impossible not to applaud. Charles, who was almost in pain from laughing, joined the others clapping.

As the noise subsided into scattered gasps and deep breaths, a strange stillness came over the room. Christopher Milton was still the focus of attention, but the mood had changed. Everyone watched him as he sat up, but he did not seem to be aware of them. He rose pensively to his feet, and moved slowly forward. 'I think we can do more with that,' he said.

The remark did not seem to be addressed to anyone in particular, but David Meldrum, as director, felt that he should pick it up. 'What do you mean, Christopher?'

'I mean there's not enough happening on stage in that number.'

'Well, of course, we haven't got the dancers yet, and the—'

'Shut up. I'm thinking.' He said it dismissively, as if he were swatting a fly. Then slowly: 'We need more movement from me, bobbing up all over the place....Yes, we need doubles.'

'Doubles?'

'Yes, doubles for me. People my height, dressed in the same costume. So that I can disappear behind one tree and appear behind another, come out of trap doors. Really make it into a silent film sequence.'

'But it works very well like this and—'

'I told you to shut up. That's how we're going to do it. The whole thing will have to be replotted.'

'But we haven't got time.'

'We'll make time.'

'Look, it's a tight rehearsal schedule—'

'Sod the rehearsal schedule. We can reblock this tomorrow afternoon.'

'We're meant to be doing the Young Marlow/Kate scenes tomorrow.'

'You can do those on Friday.'

'No,' Mark Spelthorne's voice drawled out. 'I can't do Friday. I'm released for the day. Doing a pilot of a radio series.'

'You're contracted here.'

'Agent cleared the release, Christopher old boy.'

'I don't care what your sodding agent's done. You're contracted here.'

'Listen, it's a pilot of my own show.'

'Your own show. Huh.' The laugh was loaded with scorn. 'A pilot for your own show. I wouldn't bother.

Don't do it. It'll save you disappointment when they turn the idea down.'

'What do you mean?'

'I mean that you'll never have a show of your own. You haven't got it in you. Adequate, you are. The word adequate was invented to describe people like you.'

'What the hell do you mean?' Mark had risen sharply, as if he were about to strike his antagonist. Christopher Milton looked at him with contempt.

There was a long pause. Then Mark Spelthorne backed away. He muttered, 'Bloody prima donna' in an unsuccessful tone of defiance, and walked out of the room.

A long silence followed. Everyone except Christopher Milton looked horribly embarrassed. But they all waited for him to speak first.

When he did, it was as if the argument had never happened, as if he had just been thinking. 'We'll reblock this Chase Scene tomorrow afternoon.'

'Yes,' agreed David Meldrum. 'Fine.'

Charles was glad when the rehearsals were over that day. The atmosphere was uncomfortable, although Christopher Milton seemed oblivious of it.

By chance, Charles found himself leaving at the same time as the star. They walked out of the Welsh Dragon Club in silence. Charles felt ill at ease, as though he were about to be asked to take sides, to say what he thought of Mark Spelthorne.

But that was not at all what happened. As they emerged from the Club, Christopher Milton was suddenly surrounded by small boys from the tower blocks opposite. One of them must have seen the star go in earlier in the day and spread the word. They were a rough lot, of various colours and degrees of scruffiness. They all clamoured up to Christopher Milton with scraps of paper for autographs.

As the kids moved in, a stocky figure in a dark suit detached himself from a parked Rolls Corniche and moved forward as if anticipating trouble. A gesture from

Christopher Milton stopped him and he moved back to lean against the metallic brown flank of the car.

'All right, all right. Who's first?' The voice was instantly that of Lionel Wilkins.

It was exactly what the audience wanted. They all howled with laughter and clamoured even louder for autographs. 'All right, all right. Give me a pen,' whined Lionel Wilkins. A biro was thrust into his hands. He dropped it with a distinctive Wilkins gesture. The audience howled again.

'All right. You first. What's your name?'

'Mahendra Patel.'

The timing was immaculate. An eyebrow shot up, the mouth dropped open and Lionel Wilkins said, 'I beg yours?'

The catch-phrase produced screams of delight and the little crowd jostled and shouted as their hero signed all the grubby comics, pages torn out of school books, and cigarette packets they thrust at him. He was punctilious about getting every name right and signed nearly thirty, by the time he had supplied sisters and cousins (and a few imaginary sisters and cousins to be sold at school for profit).

Eventually, they were all done. With a few more Lionel Wilkins lines and a demonstration of the Lionel Wilkins walk, Christopher Milton edged towards the back door of the Corniche. The driver opened it smartly and the star was inside. The electric window came down and the cabaret continued. The car started, the kids shouted louder, Christopher Milton waved, called out, 'Cheerio, Charles, see you tomorrow,' and the car drew away.

Charles had felt awkward during the autograph session. He didn't want to sneak off quietly, nor to come too much into the centre of things in case it looked as if he wanted to be asked for his signature too. But now Christopher Milton had drawn attention to him by mentioning his name, he felt the focus of a dozen pairs of questioning eyes.

He made a vague wave in their direction and started to turn hoping something wouldn't happen.

It did. Two little Indian boys, Mahendra Patel and a younger brother, came towards him. 'May I have your autograph?' asked the elder in perfect Cockney.

'Oh, you don't want it.' He tried to laugh it off, but the lolly wrapper which had been thrust forward was not withdrawn. Blushing furiously, he signed. The other boys stood and stared. With an ineffectual cheery wave, he gave the paper to Mahendra. Then he turned and hurried away. But not fast enough to avoid hearing the little Cockney voice say, 'No, it isn't him.'

He drank rather more than he should have done that evening at his depressing local in Westbourne Grove. He felt emotionally raw, on the edge of depression for the first time since the rehearsals had started. And, as he knew from experience, when he felt in that mood, things got out of proportion.

The afternoon's flare-up had left a nasty taste. It cast doubt on the whole atmosphere of the show. Charles realised the fragility of what he had taken to be such a good company spirit. Maybe he had condemned himself to nine months of unnecessary unpleasantness.

But after the third large Bell's he felt more able to analyse what had happened at the rehearsal. All Christopher Milton had done was to be rude to David Meldrum and Mark Spelthorne. In a good cause—he had only been thinking of improving the show. And David Meldrum's passivity positively invited rudeness. So did the affectations of that little tit Mark Spelthorne. In fact, all Christopher Milton had done was to express the opinions held by most of the cast. In fact, he had shown pretty good judgement in his choice of butts.

Having rationalised that, Charles felt better. He went and got another large Bell's.

The next day Christopher Milton was all over the *Sun* newspaper. 'It's Nightshirt Week in the Sun!' said the front page and the centrespread was a large photograph of the star in a long Dickensian nightshirt and drooping nightcap, holding a candle. He wore the familiar Lionel Wilkins expression of appalled surprise.

When it comes to nightwear, Christopher Milton, better known as Lionel Wilkins, says a nightshirt's the answer—so long as it's a long one. 'Otherwise you get very cold round the...round the...um, er...round the middle of the night. It's no fun waking up in December with your nightie round your neck.' 34-year-old Christopher is currently rehearsing a big new musical, *Lumpkin!*, which opens in the West End late November. 'The part I'm playing's a bit different from Lionel Wilkins. Tony Lumpkin's a chap who likes making trouble for everyone—oh yes, he's always getting the girls into trouble—Ooh, that's not what I meant. I beg yours!' With lovable Christopher Milton around, *Lumpkin!* should be a show worth seeing.

Lovable Christopher Milton's behaviour at rehearsals became more erratic. There were more breaks in the flow, more orders to David Meldrum to shut up, more long pauses while he worked out how a comic effect should be achieved. It was intolerable behaviour on the part of a professional actor, and yet Charles could forgive it, because he was gaining an increasing respect for the man's theatrical instinct. Christopher Milton was always right, he knew what would work for an audience. And, given David Humdrum's total lack of this quality, *Lumpkin!* needed some inspiration.

But it wasn't popular with the rest of the cast, because Christopher Milton's comic instinct was only applied to his own part. The rest of the action was hurried through and substantial cuts were suggested. Only occasionally would there be a long discussion about one of the straight scenes, and that was only if the opportunity was seen for another entrance by Tony Lumpkin.

'Um, Christopher....'

'Shut up, David. I'm thinking.'

'Look, we want to get on with this first meeting between Young Marlow and Kate.'

'Yes, I was thinking it might be better if Tony Lumpkin overheard this scene. I could be behind the screen and. . . .'

'Oh, for God's sake,' snapped Mark Spelthorne. 'This is one of the most famous scenes in English drama. It would make nonsense of the plot if Lumpkin overheard it. It wouldn't add anything.'

Christopher Milton did not seem to hear the objection; he was still working the scene out in his own mind. 'I mean, it's not a very interesting scene, no jokes or anything. I think it could be improved with Lumpkin there.'

Mark Spelthorne grew apopleptic. 'That's a load of absolute balls!'

'Um, Christopher,' said David Meldrum tentatively, 'I think we probably will be better off doing the scene as it is.'

'Hmm.' Again he was distant, still mentally planning. There was a long pause. 'I'll have a look at it.' He moved from the centre of the stage, picked up his script and sat quietly in a corner looking at it. The rehearsals continued.

Such confrontations were not conducive to good feeling. Griff's bar became a centre of disaffection and at any time of day there would be a little knot of actors there discussing their latest grievance against the star. Mark Spelthorne was always one of the most vociferous. 'I mean, let's face it, when Goldsmith wrote the play, he intended Young Marlow to be the hero. There's no question about that. Which was why I took the part. Of course, my bloody agent didn't check the script, just assumed that I would be playing the lead. At least one has the comfort that all this mucking about with the show is making a complete nonsense of it. It'll never run. Doubt if we'll actually come in, die quietly on the tour, I shouldn't wonder. And that won't do a great deal for the career of Mr Christopher Milton. Maybe teach him the dangers of over-exposure.'

'I don't know, Mark. He doesn't actually do that much work. He's very selective in what he does. Anyway, you can't talk. You're doing plenty yourself.'

'Oh yes, that's always a danger if one's popular. Have

to watch it. I mean, no doubt there'll be another series of
The Fighter Pilots. And then if this radio takes off....'

'Oh yes, that was the pilot show. How did it go?'

'Bloody marvellous. Really went a bomb. The
planners'll be fools to themselves if they turn that one
down. So I suppose I'll be stuck with doing a series of that
early next year. Not that I mind. I mean, radio doesn't
take long and in fact I have quite an affection for it. The
main thing is it's comedy, and really comedy's my best
thing. The radio might persuade the telly boys how good I
am at it. That's the trouble in telly, they do so like to
pigeon-hole people. After this *Fighter Pilots* thing, they
seem to think I'm only good for the handsome young hero
type, whereas of course....'

There were plenty of others in the company with
complaints about Christopher Milton, but Charles put it
down to the ordinary ineffectual bitching of actors. No
one seemed sufficiently motivated to want to sabotage the
show. As time went on, Gerald's fears seemed more and
more insubstantial.

It was on the Tuesday of the fourth week of rehearsals
that Charles began to wonder. By then the scale of the
production had got larger. The dancers had joined the
company, though they kept somewhat aloof in their
self-contained, camp little world. None of them had
identifiable parts, except for the prettiest girl who had
been given the wordless rôle of Bet Bouncer. There had
also been a music rehearsal with the full orchestra ('We
can't afford more than one with the band, because of the
expense'), and the musicians added another element of an
alien culture. The rehearsals became more concerned with
details. There were constant discussions with Derbyshire
Wilkes, the designer, and Spike, the stage manager, about
exact sizes of parts of the set. The pieces of tape which
marked their outlines were constantly rearranged. Actors
were continually being rushed off in taxis for final
costume fittings. The whole production was building up
to its first appearance in a theatre on the Saturday week.
On that day, their last in London before the tour,

Lumpkin! was going to have a run on an improvised set in the King's Theatre.

The presence of the augmented company did not stop Christopher Milton's continual interruption of rehearsals while he worked out new entrances and business for Tony Lumpkin. His fits of temperament did not worry the dancers or musicians. Both were well used to hanging around at the whim of whoever happened to be in charge. Whether the break was for a broken microphone or a tantrum did not make a lot of difference to them. They just waited impassively until it was time to continue. And the male dancers had a stage-struck camp affection for stardom. They would have felt cheated if Christopher Milton hadn't behaved like a star.

On the Tuesday they were rehearsing the closer (that is, the last new song of the show, not the acres of reprises which followed it). It was called *Never Gonna Marry You* ('gonna' was a favourite word in Micky Gordon's lyrics) and it sewed up the Lumpkin side of the plot by getting him out of marriage to his cousin and into marriage with Bet Bouncer (while, incidentally, leaving the rest of the plot totally unresolved). It was the only moment in the show when Charles had to sing, which was a great relief to him. Just one couplet and he was quite pleased with it. The lines rose above the general level of Micky Gorton's wit.

> '*Marriage is like a hot bath, I confess—*
> *The longer you're in it, the colder it gets.*'

It probably wasn't an original line and it didn't rhyme properly, but it was a line that would get a laugh, and that was quite a bonus to an actor in a supporting rôle. Charles cherished it; it was the only laugh he stood to get in the show.

After he had sung the couplet in rehearsal that Tuesday, there was a long pause. Christopher Milton had the next line, but he let the music continue and was silent. He looked at Charles with the preoccupied expression he always wore when he was working something out. As the accompaniment died down to untidy silence, he spoke. 'You know, that line will probably get a laugh.'

'I hope so,' said Charles cheerily. 'Unless I cock it up.'

'Hmm. I think I ought to sing it.'

'I beg your pardon.'

'I think I ought to have the line rather than you.'

'What?' Charles was stunned by the directness of the approach. He was a fairly easy-going actor and didn't make scenes over minor details as a rule, but the brazenness of this took him off his guard. 'Oh, come on, Christopher, you can't have all the laughs in the show.'

'I think I should have that line.' Christopher Milton's voice had the familiar distant quality of previous encounters with other actors whose parts he had raided.

'But it strikes me, Christopher, that that line would come much more naturally from Old Marlow, the man of the world, than from Tony Lumpkin, who, let's face it, is meant to be fairly uneducated and—'

'I think I should sing it.'

'Look, I'm not claiming that I'd deliver it better than you or anything. It's just that—'

'Huh.' The laugh came out with great savagery. 'I should think not. You'd hardly expect great delivery of lines from a tired old piss-artist. I'm sure there are lots of actors who get through their careers with your level of *competence*, but don't you start comparing yourself with me.'

The suddenness of the attack hurt like a blow in the face. Charles tried some acid line about people who felt they should have all the lines and about acting being a team effort, but it misfired. He appealed to David Meldrum for a decision and—surprise, surprise—David thought Christopher Milton probably had got a point.

Charles spent the rest of the day's rehearsal in a state of silent fury. He knew that his face was white and he was hardly capable of speech. He felt sick with anger.

As soon as he was released, he got a taxi back to Bayswater. Too churned up even for the distant conviviality of the pub, he stopped at an off licence on the way and went back to his room with a bottle of Scotch.

The room in Hereford Road was an untidy and depressing mess, with grey painted cupboards and yellow candlewick on the unmade bed. Its atmosphere usually reduced him to a state of instant depression, but on this occasion it had too much anger to compete with and he hardly noticed his surroundings. He just sat and drank solidly until there was a slight shift in his mood and he could think of something other than his fury.

It was only a line, after all. Not even a particularly good line at that. And the show was hardly one that was very important to him or one that was going to make any difference to what was laughingly called his career. It wasn't like him to get so upset over a detail.

And then he began to realise the power of Christopher Milton's personality. From his own over-reactions Charles understood the intensity of resentment that the man could inspire. Which made him think that perhaps there were people who felt sufficiently strongly to sabotage any show Christopher Milton was in.

Charles decided that he would make a belated start to the business of investigation for which Gerald Venables had engaged him. Since he had no rehearsals the following morning, he would go and see Everard Austick.

Five...

EVERARD AUSTICK'S ADDRESS was a block of flats in Eton College Road, near Chalk Farm Underground Station. Charles found it in the phone book and went along on the off-chance that its owner would be out of hospital. He could have rung to check, but felt disinclined to explain his enquiries on the telephone. Also there was a chance that the dry agony of his hangover might have receded by the time he got there.

In fact the tube journey didn't help much and, as he stood in the old lift gazing ahead at its lattice-work metal door, he felt in need of a red-hot poker to burn out the rotten bits of his brain. The only coherent thought he could piece together was the eternal, 'Must drink less'.

The block of flats was old, with long gloomy corridors interrupted by the stranded doormats of unwelcoming doorways. Number 108 was indistinguishable from the others, the same blue gloss paint, the same glass peep-hole to warn the inmate of approaching burglars, rapists, etc.

Charles' pressure on the door-bell produced no reaction. Perhaps it wasn't working. He pressed again, his ear to the door, and caught the distant rustle of its ring. Oh well, maybe Everard was still in hospital, or away convalescing. One more try.

This time there was a distant sound of a door opening, a muttered curse and the heavy approach of a plaster-cased foot. The door opened and Everard Austick peered blearily out into the shadows of the corridor. He looked a

mess. His grey hair stuck out in a series of Brylcreemed
sheaves as he had slept on it. He had only shaved sketchily
for a few days and the areas he had missed sprouted long
bristles. A dilapidated camel dressing-gown was bunched
around his large frame. His right leg was grotesquely
inflated by its plaster. He was probably only in his fifties,
but he looked an old man.

'Can I help you?' he asked in a public school voice
furred with alcohol.

'Yes. I'm sorry to trouble you. My name's Charles
Paris.'

Fuddled incomprehension.

'We worked together once for a season in Glasgow.'

'Ah. Ah yes, of course.' But he didn't remember.

'Look, I've taken over the part you were playing in
Lumpkin!'

'Oh. Do you want to come in?'

'Thank you.' Everard Austick backed away and
Charles moved past him into the dim hall. A door gave off
on to a large sitting-room and he made towards it. 'Er, not
in there if you don't mind.'

Charles had seen the smart decor of the room and
looked back quizzically at Everard. 'Fact is, old boy, I
don't use all the flat. No point in using it all when I'm
away so much . . . I . . . er, there's a young couple who also
live here. Just on a temporary basis. Helps out with the
old rent, what?' The jovial tone could not hide the facts.
Everard Austick was so hard up that he had to rent out
almost all his flat to keep his head above water.

This impression was confirmed when Charles was led
into Everard's bedroom, obviously the smallest in the flat.
The air tasted as if it hadn't been changed for a fortnight.
A pile of dusty magazines against them showed that the
windows hadn't been opened for months, and the bed was
rumpled not just by one night's occupation, but by long
days and nights of simply lying and staring at the ceiling
rose.

A half-empty bottle of vodka on the dressing-table was
evidence of the only activity the room had seen for some
time. 'Sorry it's a bit of a tip,' said Everard, attempting to

play the line with light comedy insouciance. 'Can I offer you a drink? There's only the vodka, I'm afraid. Well, I suppose I could make some coffee, but. . . .' His mind was unable to cope with the incongruity of the idea.

'A little vodka would be fine.' A hair of the dog might possibly loosen the nutcrackers on Charles' head.

He received a clouded toothmug half-full of vodka . . . Everard Austick's hand shook as he passed it over and topped up his own tumbler. 'Down the hatch, old boy.' The long swallow he took was not an action of relish, but of dependence. He grimaced, shuddered and looked at Charles. 'Now, what can I do for you, old man? Want a bit of help in your interpretation of the part, eh?' Again the cheerfulness sounded forced.

'No, actually I just wanted to pick your brains about something.' Charles paused. It was difficult. He did not want to reveal his rôle as an investigator into the show. He realised that he had not done enough preparation for the encounter; he should have worked out some specious story to explain his interest, or even made the approach in some other identity. Still, too late now. Better to try the direct question and hope that Everard's bemused condition would prevent him from being suspicious. 'You know when you broke your leg—what happened?'

'I fell down the stairs.'

'Just an accident?'

'Oh, God knows. I'd had quite a skinful the night before, met a few chums, celebrating actually being in work, it had been a long time. And I had a few more in the morning, you know, to pull me round, and I managed to leave late, so I was hurrying, so I suppose I could have just fallen.'

'Or?'

'Well, there was this chap on the stairs, ran down from behind me, I thought he sort of jostled me. I don't know though.'

'And that's what caused you to fall?'

'Could have been. I don't know.'

'Did he stop to help you when you fell?'

'No, he seemed to be in a hurry.'

'Hmm. Did you see what he looked like?'

'No.'

'Not even an impression?'

'Nothing.'

'Did you tell the police?'

'No. Who's going to believe me? I'm not even sure it happened myself. Could just have fallen.'

'Yes.' The interrogation did not seem to be getting anywhere. Everard Austick was so fogged with alcohol that he didn't even trust his own memory. No one was going to get anything else out of him. Charles drained his glass and rose to leave.

'You're off?' Everard seemed to accept the departure with as little surprise as he had the arrival. Nothing seemed strange in his half-real world. 'Actually, there is one thing, old boy.'

'Yes?'

'This damned leg, I find it so difficult to get about, you know, get to the bank and so on, a bit short of cash, for the ... er ... you know, basic necessities of life.'

The expansive gesture which accompanied the last four words was meant to signify a whole range of food and domestic essentials, but it ended up pointing at the nearly-empty vodka bottle.

Out of guilt or something, Charles gave him a fiver. Then a thought struck him. 'Everard, why didn't you use the lift that morning?'

'Wasn't working.'

'Sure?'

'I pushed the button for it and it didn't come for a long time. I told you I was in a hurry.'

'Yes. Thank you.'

Charles walked slowly along the dim corridor until he came to the lifts. He looked at them closely. Both were the old sort with sliding doors. A notice requested users to close both doors firmly. Otherwise the lifts would not function. So it would be possible to immobilise both by calling them to another floor and leaving them with their doors ajar. It would then be possible to linger in the gloomy corridor until Everard Austick staggered out of his flat, watch him call unsuccessfully for the lift and then help him on his way when he started downstairs. Unlikely, but possible.

'Hello, Gerald, it's Charles. I got your message at the rehearsal rooms and I'm afraid this is the first chance I've had to call.'

'Okay. How's it going?'

'Nothing to report really. Nothing else has happened.'

'No tension in the company?'

'No more than in any show with Christopher Milton in it which starts its pre-London tour in a week.'

'Hmm. Maybe I was being alarmist.'

'Maybe. Anyway, thanks for the job.'

'Any time. Keep your eyes skinned.'

'Okay. Though I don't know what for. There's nothing to see.'

'Unless something else happens.'

'Hello, is that Ruth?'

'Yes. Who's speaking?'

'Charles Paris.'

'Good God. I thought the earth had swallowed you up long ago.'

'No. Still large as life and twice as seedy.'

'Well, to what do I owe this pleasure? Tidying out your room and just found a seven-year-old diary?'

'No.'

'Joined Divorcees Anonymous have you, they gave you my number?'

'Actually I'm still not divorced.'

'Separated though?'

'Oh yes.'

'And you just phoned for the Recipe-of-the-Day, did you? It's stew.'

'No, the fact is, I'm in a show that's about to start a pre-London tour and our first week's in Leeds and, with true actor's instinct, I thought, well, before I fix up any digs, I'll see if I've got any old friends in Leeds. . . .'

'You've got a nerve.'

'Sorry, I shouldn't have asked. I'll—'

'No. It might be quite entertaining to see you after all these years. At least a change from the sort of men who hang around divorcees in Leeds. When do you arrive?'

'Sunday.'

As Charles put the phone down, Ruth's voice still rang, ominously familiar, in his ears and he had the feeling that he had done something stupid.

If all went well on the tour, *Lumpkin!* was to take over the King's Theatre from a show called *Sex of One and Half a Dozen of the Other*, which had long outstayed its welcome. It had been put on in 1971 by Marius Steen and had celebrated a thousand performances just before the impresario's mysterious death in which Charles Paris had become involved. As the Steen empire was slowly dismantled, the show had continued under different managements with increasingly diluted casts until even the coach party trade began to dwindle. It limped through the summer of 1975 on tourists, but had no chance of surviving the pre-Christmas slump. The theatre-going public had been too depressed by rising ticket prices and the fear that the terrorist bombs might return with the dark evenings to make the effort to see a tired old show. *Sex of One . . .* had made its London killing and was now off to pick up the residuals of national tours, the depredations of provincial theatre companies and finally the indignities perpetrated by amateur dramatic societies.

On Saturday, October 25th, the last day of London rehearsals, the *Lumpkin!* cast assembled for a pre-tour run-through in the King's. The idea was to gain familiarity with the place before the ceremonial entry on November 27th.

The call was for nine o'clock, so that everything should be ready when Christopher Milton arrived at his contractual ten-thirty. Time was tight. *Sex of One . . .* had a three o'clock matinée and their set (most of which had been dismantled and piled up against the naked brick walls at the back of the stage) had to be reassembled by two-thirty. This meant that an eleven o'clock start would

just allow a full run, with only half an hour allowed for
cock-ups.

The run was not to be with costume or props.
Everything had been packed up into skips and was
already on its way to Leeds. The set was in lorries on the
M1, scheduled to arrive for the get-in at ten-thirty that
night when the current show at the Palace Theatre (a
second-rate touring revival of *When We Are Married*)
finished its run. Spike, the stage manager, was going to
see the run-through, then leap on to the five to four train
to Leeds and maybe grab a little sleep in anticipation of
the all-night and all-day job of getting the set erected and
dressed. The actors' schedule was more leisurely. After
the run, their next call was at seven o'clock on the Sunday
evening for a technical rehearsal. At eleven the next
morning there was a press conference in the bar of the
Palace Theatre, a dress rehearsal at one, and at
seven-thirty on Monday, October 27th, *Lumpkin!* was to
meet a paying audience for the first time.

The audience in the King's Theatre on the Saturday
morning had not paid. They were all in the circle. David
Meldrum, with a rare display of personality, had taken
over all of the stalls and set up a little table in the middle.
A Camping Gaz lamp was ready to illuminate his
interleaved script and notes when the lights went down.
Two chairs were set there, one for him and one for
Gwyneth, ever efficient, never passing comment.

Up in the circle were some of the backers, who joked
nervously like race-horse owners, frightened of coughs,
lameness and nobbling. Dickie Peck was there, salivating
over his cigar until it looked like a rope-end. There was a
representative of Amulet Productions, who looked as if
he had gone to a fancy-dress ball as a merchant banker.
Gerald Venables was too cool to turn up himself and
reveal his anxiety, but a junior member of the office was
there representing the interests of Arthur Balcombe.
Some other seats were occupied by Press representatives
and a few girl and boy friends who had been smuggled in.

The stage manager had imposed dress rehearsal
discipline and the cast were not allowed out front. Nor

were they encouraged to make themselves at home in the dressing-rooms, so there was a lot of hanging around in the green room and the wings. Charles decided that once the run started he would adjourn to the nearest pub. Even with a totally trouble-free run, Sir Charles Marlow could not possibly be required onstage until one o'clock. He knew he should really hang about the green room listening to the gossip and trying to cadge a lift up to Leeds. But he hated cadging and would rather actually spend the travel allowance he had received on a train ticket than try it.

He listened to the beginning of the run-through on the Tannoy. It sounded pretty pedestrian. He left a message as to his where abouts with one of the stage management and started towards the pub.

But just as he was leaving the green room, he met Mark Spelthorne. 'Good God, Charles, it's pitch dark out there on the stage. There's just some basic preset and no working lights on in the wings. I just tripped over something and went headlong.'

'What did you trip over?' he asked, suddenly alert.

'Don't know. Something just by the back exit from the stage.'

Charles moved quietly in the dark behind the black tabs which represented the limits of the *Lumpkin!* set. He had a chilly feeling that he was about to discover something unpleasant.

His foot touched a soft shape. Soft cloth. He knelt down in the dark and put his hands forward reluctantly to feel what it was.

Just at that moment someone became aware of the lack of light backstage and switched on working lights. Charles screwed up his eyes against the sudden brightness, then opened them and looked down.

It was a cushion. A large scatter cushion, part of the set dressing for *Sex of One . . .*, which had been dropped when the set was cleared. Charles felt sheepish and looked round, embarrassed. He was alone. He shut off the flow of melodramatic thoughts which had been building in his head.

Still, he was there in a watchdog capacity. Better safe

than sorry, he argued in self-justification. To reinforce this illusion of purpose he went across to the pile of tall, heavy flats leant haphazardly against the brick wall. They did not look very safe, some nearly vertical, some almost overhanging. He inspected more closely. Oh, it was all right, there was a pair of thick ropes crossed over the flats, restraining them. They were fixed to rings at the top and the loose ends were wound firmly round a large wooden cleat on the wall. No danger there. Charles tried not to feel a fool and went off to the pub.

That morning's run-through had all the animation of a bus queue. Nothing went wrong, but, God, it was dull. Everyone seemed to feel this and there was a great sag as they came to the end of the final reprise. 'Excellent,' said David Meldrum's voice from somewhere near the Camping Gaz glow. 'Two hours, fifty-seven minutes,' as if the stopwatch were the only criterion of theatrical excellence. 'Right, well done, everybody. Now we must clear the theatre as soon as possible. I've got one or two notes on that run, but I'll give them to you before the Tech. run on Sunday. Okay. See you all in Leeds. That run was really super, loves.'

The cast, who didn't agree and didn't think saying 'loves' suited him, dispersed grumbling. There was a communal feeling of apathetic gloom. The *Sex of One* . . . stage crew came onstage to start rebuilding their set for a few coachloads of sweet-paper-rustling pensioners. Dickie Peck arrived and started to talk in an undertone to Christopher Milton. The star's driver, who had also appeared from somewhere, stood at a respectful distance. The cast hurried off to tie up the loose ends of their shopping, or sex lives, which had to be done before they left London. Charles made for the exit.

It was at that moment that all the working lights went out again. This was greeted by the usual curses and cheap jokes. Then suddenly there was another sound, an ominous heavy scrape of wood. It merged into a thud and a scream of pain. Voices, suddenly serious, shouted, 'Lights!'

The working lights revealed a silent tableau. The pile of

flats had toppled forward from the wall and lay almost flat on the ground. Protruding from under them was the torso of Mark Spelthorne. Christopher Milton, his driver and Dickie Peck were frozen where the flats had just missed them. Other members of the cast and stage crew stood aghast.

Suddenly everyone rushed forward and started heaving at the wood and canvas to lift it off Mark's body.

'It's all right,' came the familiar drawl. 'Don't fret.'

The helpers stood back as Mark extricated himself. He stood up and rubbed his shoulder.

'Are you all right?'

'I think I'll have a bit of a bruise tomorrow, but otherwise, fine.'

'God, you were lucky,' said Spike, who was looking at where the top edges of the flats had come to rest. 'Look.'

The wall had been Mark's salvation. Because the flats had been a little longer than the floor on which they fell, they had been stopped short when they met the wall, which had taken their weight. Scraping and chipping on the brick showed the force with which they had fallen.

'No one else under there, is there?'

Spike crouched and looked into the triangle of darkness under the flats. After what seemed a long time he straightened up. 'No. Look, could some of you lads help me to get these back?'

'Certainly. Let me give a hand.' Mark Spelthorne, having inadvertently been cast in the rôle of hero, continued to play it.

'That could have been a very nasty accident,' said Christopher Milton.

'All in a day's work for Flying Officer Falconer of *The Fighter Pilots*,' said Mark Spelthorne smugly.

'Whoever tied up those flats should get his cards,' Spike grunted with professional disgust.

'Don't know who did it,' mumbled one of the *Sex of One* . . . crew.

'Oh well. It happened, not much we can do about it now,' said one of the dancers brightly. 'Don't want to cry over spilt milk, do we? Just mop it up and squeeze the rag back into the bottle, eh?'

This seemed to break the atmosphere. They all helped to push the flats against the wall again and went off laughing and chatting.

Except for Charles Paris. He had seen how firmly the restraining ropes had been fixed to the cleat. He knew what had happened had not been an accident.

PART 2

Leeds

Six . . .

ON THE TRAIN up to Leeds that Sunday afternoon Charles cursed his lack of detective instinct. He had been present at what was probably a crime and just when his mind should be flashing up an instant recall of every detail of the scene it was providing only vague memories and woolly impressions. Perhaps it was Oliver Goldsmith's fault. By delaying Sir Charles Marlow's entry until the fifth act, he had ensured that Charles Paris had had at least two pints too many at the Saturday lunchtime, so that the ideal computer print-out of facts and details was replaced by a child's picture in Fuzzy Felt.

He couldn't even remember exactly who had been there. Christopher Milton, certainly, and Dickie Peck and the driver. And David Meldrum and Gwyneth were somewhere around, though he couldn't remember whether they were on stage or in the auditorium at the time of the accident. Mark Spelthorne had been there, of course, and Spike and some of the King's Theatre stage staff. . . . And then who else? Two or three male dancers—Charles didn't know their names, but he'd recognise them again—and the two girl dancers. Then one or two of the supporting actors and actresses. Charles screwed up his eyes and tried to see the scene again. Lizzie Dark certainly, she'd been there, and Michael Peyton, and some others. The edges of the picture were cloudy.

'Damn!' he snapped, and opened his eyes to find that

the word had attracted the gaze of a large Bradford-bound Pakistani family. Embarrassed, he closed his eyes and tried to concentrate again. A little chill of anxiety about seeing Ruth kept getting in the way.

Well, the identity parade of suspects wasn't very impressive, because it was incomplete. But, assuming a crime had been committed, it must have a motive and that might give a clue to the criminal.

The first question—was Mark Spelthorne the intended victim or was it just chance that caught him? Christopher Milton was not far behind and it was possible that the criminal was after him, but misjudged his timing in the dark. Or it could have been meant for any one of the people on stage. Or just a random blow for whoever happened to be there. The last would tie in with Gerald's original view that someone was trying to wreck the show and didn't mind how. If it was a personal vendetta against Christopher Milton, then why had the perpetrator bothered to make his first attacks on the pianist and Everard Austick? Why not go straight to his quarry? And why not use a more selective method than a tumbling pile of flats? If, on the other hand, Mark Spelthorne was the intended victim. . . .

Oh dear. He knew it wasn't getting him anywhere. Any of the people on stage at the time of the accident could have unwound the rope from the cleat. Equally, any of them could have been the intended victim. And since he couldn't remember exactly who had been there, the possibilities were infinite. Add the difficulty of tying the motivation for that crime in with the other two and the problem was insoluble, or at least insoluble to a forty-eight-year-old actor who had spent too long in the bar at King's Cross and who was having serious misgivings about going to stay with a woman with whom he had had a brief and not wholly glorious affair seven years previously.

He looked out of the window at the matt flatness of the Midlands. He closed his eyes, but sleep and even relaxation kept their distance. A new question formed in his mind—Did the 15.10 train from King's Cross to Leeds have a bar? He set out to investigate.

Ruth was disagreeable. As soon as he saw her again he remembered. Not disagreeable in the sense of being unattractive; her trim body with its sharp little breasts and well-defined calf muscles remained as good as ever; she was disagreeable in the sense that she disagreed with everything one said. Charles never had known whether it was a genuine defence from a reasoned feminist standpoint or sheer bloody-mindedness. But it came back to him as soon as she spoke. Her voice was marinated in cynicism. Charles felt a great swoop of despair, as if all his worst opinions of himself were suddenly ratified, as if the thoughts that infected him in his lowest moods had suddenly been classified as gospel. He saw himself as an Everard Austick, an alcoholic whose failure in his chosen profession was only matched by his failure as a human being.

It wasn't that cynicism struck no chord. He himself tended to attribute the worst motives to everyone and was distrustful of optimists. But like all practitioners of an art, he liked to feel that his version of it was a definitive one. His cynicism could still be unexpectedly erased by the sight of a child or the shock of a sudden kindness or a moment of desire, while Ruth's blanket coverage seemed to debase the currency of cynicism.

It wasn't that she'd had a particularly bad life. True, its emotional path had been a bit rocky. In her twenties she had had a series of affairs which never stood a chance of going the distance (Charles would have put himself in that category) and eventually at the age of thirty married a central heating systems salesman five years her senior. The marriage lasted three years until he went off with a croupier and they got a divorce. The fatalism with which Ruth accepted this reverse suggested that she had never had much faith in the marriage and had been undermining it for some time.

'So you came.' She spoke with that exactness of

enunciation which is more revealing than an accent.

'Yes, I said I would.'

'Oh yes.' The disbelief in her tone instantly put the clock back seven years. 'And how are you, Mr Charles Paris?'

'Fine, fine.'

'Good. And your lady wife?'

'I don't know. Well, when I last saw her. It's a few months back now. I believe she has a boy friend, someone from the school where she teaches.'

'Good for her. Not going to wait forever on your filing system, is she? Can I get you a cup of tea or a drink or something? Or should I show you up to your room in true landlady fashion?' She leant against the kitchen table in a way that could have been meant to be provocative. It was always difficult to know with Ruth. But seeing her, Charles remembered how much he had fancied her. That was really all there ever had been to the relationship. If there were nothing to life except bed, they'd still have been together. He felt a warm trickle of desire in spite of all the gloom which she had generated inside him.

He overcompensated by the heartiness of his reply. 'A cup of tea would be really... grand.' Her flash of suspicion made him wish he had chosen another word. He'd forgotten how sensitive she was to anything that could be construed as criticism of her Yorkshireness.

She made the tea and Charles kept up a relentless flow of banter to stop himself from making a pass at her. 'How are things in Headingley then?'

'They don't change. I've lived here thirty-four years and lost hope that they ever will.'

'Still in the same job?'

'Oh yes. I think Perkis and Levy, Solicitors and Commissioners for Oaths, would cease to function without my secretarial assistance.'

'Enjoy it?'

She spread open her hands in a gesture which showed up the pointlessness of the question.

'And socially?'

'Socially life here is okay if you're a teenybopper going

down the discos or an elegant blue-rinse who likes bridge and golf. I'm neither.'

'No.' The little gusts of interest which had been propelling the conversation along died down to silence. Charles was morbidly aware of the outline of Ruth's nipples through the cotton of her patterned blouse.

She broke the silence. 'This show you're doing, is it the one at the Palace?'

'Yes.'

'With Christopher Milton in it?'

'Yes.'

'He's good,' she said with more enthusiasm than usual. 'What's he like?'

The classic question, as asked by every member of the public about every star. And virtually unanswerable. No reply can possibly satisfy the questioner, who usually has only thought as far as the question.

Charles tried. 'Well, he's . . .' And then realised he could not even answer to his own satisfaction. 'I don't know.'

He was glad of the seven o'clock call at the Palace Theatre, as it temporarily took off the pressure of Ruth's presence.

After David Meldrum's tentative notes on the Saturday run-through (interrupted by less tentative ones from Christopher Milton), Charles sorted out a later call with the stage management and set off to investigate the adjacent pub.

It was small and dingy, one of the few old buildings which had survived the extensive modernization of Leeds city centre. A few regulars sat around in despairing huddles while a younger group played silent, grim darts. Charles ordered a large Bell's, which they didn't have, and got a large Haig. As he turned to find a space on one of the railway waiting-room benches, he recognised a figure in a blue donkey jacket hunched against the bar. 'Hello, Kevin.'

The bleary eyes showed that the writer had been there since opening time. Charles received an indifferent drunken greeting.

'Not a bad theatre, is it?'

'Not a bad theatre? Huh. Are you telling me about the Palace Theatre? That's good. I've been seeing shows at the Palace since I was six. Pantomimes, all sorts. I was brought up here. Meanwood. Went to the grammar school. We were always brought on outings to the Palace, when there was anything cultural on, touring companies, all that. Always came to the Palace. It was my ambition, when I was in my teens, to have something of mine done, performed at the Palace. That and losing my virginity.'

'And now I assume you've managed both.'

'One happened, near as dammit, in the back row of the Cottage Road Cinema.' He let out an abrupt, dirty laugh. Then his face darkened. 'But the other. . . .'

'The other you achieve tomorrow. First night.'

Kevin looked him straight in the eyes for a moment before he spoke. 'Oh yes. Tomorrow. First night. But first night of what? Do you think I'll feel any pride in *that*?'

'Don't worry. It's going to be a good show. It's inevitable that everyone's a bit jumpy just before it starts.' Charles had not decided yet what he really thought of the show, but he thought reassurance was required.

As it turned out, he was wrong. 'That's not what I mean. I mean that what'll go on at that theatre tomorrow will have nothing to do with me.'

'Oh, I know it's changed a bit from the original production, but that's inevitable when—'

'Changed a bit—huh! There's almost nothing in that show that I put there.'

'I'm sure a lot of it's still quite close to the original.'

'Balls. I should never have agreed. If I'd known what a total cock-up they were going to make of it . . . okay, they wanted to get in somebody else to do the music . . . all right, maybe Joe Coatley's music wasn't that commercial, but I thought at least they'd leave my text alone. I felt bad about dropping Joe at the time, but now I bloody envy him. I'd give anything to be out of it.'

Deliberately crude, Charles mentioned the money.

'Oh yes, there'll be plenty of money. Run forever, a show like this, or at least until his Lordship gets bored

with it. You know, I used to think I'd do anything for
money—that was when I hadn't got any—thought I'd
write anything, pornography, all sorts. I did, I wrote a real
hard-core porn book—filth, all about whips and Alsa-
tians, real muck. I got a hundred pounds for that, but I tell
you, I'm more proud of that than I will be when this load
of shit's running in the West End and bringing me in my so
many per cent a week.' He was in full flow, spurred on by
the drink. 'Look, I'm a writer, a writer. If I didn't want to
be a writer, I'd be some other bloody thing, an
accountant, a clerk in the Town Hall, I don't care what.
But that's not what I wanted to be. I wanted to be a writer.
And why does someone want to be a writer?'

Charles had his own views on the subject, but didn't
volunteer them. Anyway, Kevin's question turned out be
be rhetorical. 'I'll tell you why someone wants to be a
writer. Because what he writes is his own. It may be
rubbish, but it's his own rubbish. No one can take that
away from him. He wrote it.' He seemed to realise he was
becoming almost incoherently repetitive and paused to
collect his thoughts before continuing. He swayed
slightly.

'And that is why I don't like my work being destroyed
by some jumped-up idiot of an actor, who couldn't even
write his own name.'

Charles found himself (not for the first time) taking up
a position of boring middle-aged reasonableness. 'Kevin,
one has to face it that there are some things which work on
the page that don't work in performance.'

'I accept that. Good God, I've worked on plays before.
I'm used to doing rewrites and changing things and
cutting things down, but in the past it's always been a
matter of discussing it, not just some prima donna
ballsing up whole scenes so that he gets all the lines.'

Charles smarted at the remembrance of his own
suffering from Christopher Milton on a line-hunt, but
continued his defence. 'Look, I know he's got an
unfortunate manner, but he does have a real genius for the
theatre. He knows what's going to work and what—'

'He knows what's going to work for him, yes, but he

doesn't give a bugger about the rest of the show. He's
already made nonsense of the plot by cutting down the
Young Marlow scenes to nothing. The show'll be a great
shapeless mess.'

'The audience will love it.'

'Audience, huh. What the hell do they know? The
audience that comes to this show will be so force-fed with
television they won't notice what it's about. They'll spend
all their time waiting for the commercials. They'd come
and see him if he was peeling potatoes onstage. They'd
come and see anything that they saw on their screen. A jug
of water, *as featured on the Nine O'Clock News*, that's
what they'd come to see.'

He paused for breath. Charles took the opportunity to
buy more drinks, hoping to break the monologue. But
when he'd handed Kevin a large whisky, raised his own
and said 'Cheers', it was instantly resumed. 'There's a lot
of good stuff in that show which has just been dumped.
Dumped and replaced by corny rubbish. I know. I'm not
saying I'm the greatest writer there ever was, but I know
when I've written a good line, and I don't write them so
that some idiot can just come along and. . . .' He lost his
thread and when he came back his voice was cold with
concentration. 'If he takes anything else out of this show,
I'll kill the bastard. I've warned him, I've warned him that
I can get nasty, and I will. Do you know, last Friday he
was even saying he didn't know whether *Liberty Hall* was
a good number or not. *Liberty Hall*, I mean that's the best
number in the show. It's the only one they kept from the
original. They had to, they'd never get a better number
than that, would they? Go on, you say what you think of
it. Of that song.'

Charles, who hated being button-holed for opinions,
murmured something about it being a very good number.

'Too right it is. A bloody good number. I tell you, if he
tries to get rid of that song, I will kill him.'

Kevin became more violent and unintelligible as the
drink seeped in and Charles was relieved when it was time
for him to return to the theatre.

As he travelled back to Headingley in the 33 bus, he thought about Kevin. Most of it he put down to the drink, but it was another example of the violent reactions Christopher Milton inspired. Kevin had plenty of motive for wishing ill to the show, if he was really as disgusted with it as he claimed. And he had said something about having warned Christopher Milton, which could be a reference to the previous crimes. And, Charles suddenly remembered, the writer had been onstage at the King's Theatre when the flats fell. A new thought came into his mind. Suppose the first two accidents were genuine and the campaign of persecution only began with the falling flats. And suppose the object of the persecution was not the show, but just Christopher Milton. Someone hated the star so much that he wanted to kill him.

Back at the semi in Headingley Ruth had gone to bed, but her door was ajar and the light on. Charles knocked softly and went in.

She looked up without surprise. 'So you've finished.' Her voice could imbue the simplest sentence with criticism.

'Yes.' He sat heavily on the bed.

'Drunk, I suppose.'

'Moderately.'

'You're a wreck, Charles.' She said it hard, without affection. Then she reached forward and touched his hand. The scent of talcum powder rose to his nostrils. He looked at her. And then he kissed her.

She responded, as he knew she would. As he had known when he had first heard he was going to Leeds. From that moment a guilty fascination had led him to this. His unwillingness, his positive knowledge that it was idiotic to restart the affair, was swamped by animal urgency. His right hand scrabbled roughly at her nightdress, pulling it up.

'I know what you want.' Even as her hands reached down hungrily to fight with the clasp of his trousers, she made it sound like an accusation.

Seven...

IIN THE AUDIENCE at *Lumpkin!*'s first public performance on Monday, October 27th, 1975, were some people with a special interest in the show. There were the Friends of the Palace Theatre who spent the performance preparing witty things to say at the discussion with the cast which their secretary, Miss Thompson, had arranged to take place on stage after the final curtain. There were Kevin McMahon's parents whom he hadn't been able to dissuade from coming. There was Dickie Peck, just arrived from London to see that everyone was doing exactly what his protégé wanted. And there was Gerald Venables, up in theory in his legal capacity to extort money from a wealthy mill-owner, and in fact to keep an eye on his investment and get a progress report from Charles Paris.

The performance they watched was unusual, in that it started with one central character and ended with another. Charles saw it all from the fly gallery. It was strictly against theatre discipline for him to be up there, but he had asked Spike, who didn't seem to mind. Spike was easy-going about most things. He had that equable technician's temperament that never failed to amaze Charles. The ability to continue hard physical work up to seventy-two hours without ever losing his resource and surly good humour. And all without any sort of public recognition. The extrovert actor part of Charles could not understand that. What made people like Spike tick? Where did they come from?

He looked across at the intent acne-ridden face as the stage manager pulled on a thick rope and delicately eased a huge piece of scenery up between two metal bars with their heavy load of lights. Charles instantly remembered stories of flying disasters, of cumbersome pieces plummeting down on actors below, of faulty counterweighting snatching technicians up from the stage to dash them against the chipping machine of the grid in the roof. But the sight of Spike's strength and control put away such thoughts. The eternal stage manager. As the name implied, he could always manage. There was no point in thinking what Spike might have done before; it was impossible to imagine him in any other world.

As the show progressed, Charles' attention soon moved from speculations about the stage staff to the strange transformation which was taking place onstage, the transformation of the character of Tony Lumpkin. Christopher Milton's performance started as it had been in rehearsal. The knowing yokel dominated the stage, his voice deeply rustic and his movements capturing the clumsy grace of the farm-boy. Charles settled down to enjoy it.

The change, when it came, was quite abrupt. Audience reaction was a bit slow, but no slower than one would expect from a Monday night house of stuffed shirts from the clothing industry and a few stray television fans, awestruck by the unaccustomed space of a theatre. Charles had been in many shows which had got worse reaction at this tender stage of their lives.

But Christopher Milton was worried. His anxiety was not apparent to the audience, but to Charles, who knew the performance well, the fear showed. There was a hesitancy in delivery, a certain stiffness in dancing that betrayed the inward unrest. It came to a head in the *Liberty Hall* number. This involved a parodic country dance for Tony Lumpkin and the dancers. It was a well-choreographed routine, which started with heavy deliberation and speeded up until Christopher Milton was spinning giddily on a rostrum centre stage, from which he did a final jump to a kneeling position, an inevitable cue for applause.

He'd done it perfectly in rehearsal, but on the first night he mistimed it. He came out of the spin into the jump and landed untidily on one leg. It was not a serious error and certainly did not hurt him, but it was messy. The audience realised it had gone wrong, lost their own natural timing and did not come in with instantaneous applause.

The pause was tiny, the audience goodwill to clap was there, but the mistake had thrown them. Christopher Milton felt the hiatus and came in quickly with the line, 'Ooh, I done it all wrong.'

This time the reaction was enormous. An instant laugh, the loudest of the evening, which melted naturally into vigorous clapping, as if the audience wanted to make up for missing their first cue.

As a professional Charles could recognise Christopher Milton's immaculate timing of the line, but it was not that which struck him most about it. It was the voice in which it had been delivered. The star had not used his own voice, nor that of Tony Lumpkin. The line had been spoken by Lionel Wilkins of the television series *Straight up, Guv*.

And from that point on, Lionel Wilkins took over. For the next ten minutes or so, Tony Lumpkin fought a desultory rearguard action, but he was defeated before he started. The rustic burr was replaced by a London whine. The brown frock coat was thrown into the wings and the part was played in timeless shirtsleeves. Oliver Goldsmith, who had probably done a few gyrations in his grave over the previous weeks, must by now have been turning fast enough to power the National Grid. One of the central themes of his play, the contrast between Town and Country, had just vanished. The plot lost yet another of its tenuous links with sense.

And the audience loved it. Familiarity gave them the confidence they needed to express their enthusiasm. It may have been a bit difficult to follow the twists and exposition of an old-fashioned story, but to be presented with an instantly recognisable character from their television screens, that made it all simple. Charles watched from the fly gallery in amazement. 'What the hell is he doing?' he murmured to Spike, who was leaning on the rail beside him.

'His own thing,' Spike grunted. 'Never does anything else.'

'What will David Humdrum say?'

Charles knew the answer to his question, but Spike supplied it. 'He'll say, "Fine".'

And he did. Charles saw the encounter between star and director in the green room at the interval. 'Christ, this needs a lot more work,' said the star.

'It's going fine, Christopher, just fine,' soothed the director.

'That *Liberty Hall* number will have to come out for a start. I always thought it was a load of crap.'

'I'm sure, with a bit more rehearsal—'

'Shut up! It's coming out.' Christopher Milton went up to his dressing-room.

Charles decided that it was in his interests as the show's secret watchdog to keep his eyes on the movements of Kevin McMahon. If the writer lived up to half of his drunken threats, there was going to be trouble.

The trouble started as soon as the curtain had come down on the final call. Kevin McMahon was in the green room to greet the cast as they came offstage. He went straight up to Christopher Milton and shouted, 'What the hell do you mean by performing my stuff like that? This isn't one of your tatty TV comedies!'

The star seemed to look through him and greeted a man with greasy swept-back hair and a cheap suede zip-up jacket. 'Hello, Wally. What did you think?'

'Good bits, bad bits,' said Wally Wilson in broad Cockney.

'Never mind. Nothing that can't be changed.'

'Too right. Soon be up to the *Straight Up, Guv* standard!'

'Now you bloody listen to me, Mr Christopher Bloody Milton...' Kevin began belligerently.

The response came back like a whip-lash. 'Shut up, I'm talking to a writer.'

The implication was too much for Kevin McMahon.

With a cry of fury, he drew his fist back for a blow.

Christopher Milton moved fast. He sidestepped with a dancer's ease. Kevin swung himself off balance and at that moment Dickie Peck, who had moved from the doorway at amazing speed when the fracas started, flicked up Kevin's head with his left forearm and smashed a hard right knuckle into the writer's mouth. The knees gave, the body crumpled and blood welled from a cut lip. 'Don't you ever dare lay a finger on him.' Dickie Peck hissed.

The action had all been so quick that it left behind a shocked silence. The unexpectedness of the fight paled into insignificance compared to the transformation of Dickie Peck, suddenly converted from a middle-aged joke figure to a bruiser. Charles recollected a distant rumour that the agent had started his career as a boxer.

Christopher Milton broke the silence. He continued in an even tone, as if nothing had happened. 'Wally, come up to my dressing-room and have a chat.'

'Love to.' Wally's casualness was more studied.

'Um, er, Mr Milton.' A young man who had been hovering uneasily round the edges of the green room, stepped forward, blushing furiously.

'What?'

'I'm, er, um... my name is Bates and, er, I'm representing Mr Katzmann, who, as you know, is, er, the general manager of the theatre and—'

'What the hell are you burbling about?'

'Well, er, as you know, the, er... the, er. . . .' He ran out of syntax. 'The Friends.'

'Are you coming, Wally?'

'Mr Milton.' Panic made the young man articulate again, and he blurted out his message. 'The Friends of the Palace Theatre are about to hold their discussion of the show on stage and, as Mr Katzmann arranged, you and the other members of the cast will be joining in the discussion.'

'I bloody won't. It's the first I've heard of it. If you think I'm going to piss around talking crap to old ladies, you can forget it.'

'But—'

Dickie Peck cut the young man short with a gesture and again took control. 'Has this been advertised?'

'Yes. Mr Katzmann arranged it months ago.'

'Not through me, he didn't. You'd better do it, Chris.'

'Look, I've just done a bloody performance, I've just been assaulted by a lunatic hack-writer, I'm not going to—'

Dickie Peck raised his hand and the voice petered out. 'You've got to do it, Chris. It's a bloody lumber and—' with a glance at Mr Bates, who trembled visibly—'there'll be hell to pay for someone in the morning when I find out who made the cock-up. But if it's been advertised ... you can't afford to get the reputation of someone who jacks out of that sort of thing.'

Christopher Milton swore obscenely and loud, but accepted the logic of the argument. He went upstairs to take off his make-up and, as often happened when he left the room, the atmosphere relaxed. People started to drift away. Charles went across to Kevin McMahon, who had dragged himself quietly to a sofa and was dabbing at his lip with a handkerchief. 'I think it's time to take the money and run, Kevin. Put this down to bad experience. Reckon that it's just a grant of money to buy you time to go off and write what you really want to.'

'I really wanted to write *Liberty Hall*.'

'Yes, but there must be other things, more original, more your own that you want to get on with.'

'Oh yes, things where I express the real me, things that the world has been waiting to have written by some genius who only needs time to get on with it.'

Charles ignored the heaviness of the irony. 'Yes, that sort of thing.'

'Don't you patronise me!' Kevin stood up. 'I'm going to kill the bastard,' he said and walked out of the theatre.

'But,' said Mrs Crichton-Smith, whose husband owned a sock factory and played off an eight handicap, 'I remember doing *She Stoops to Conquer* at school and I must say a lot of the original plot seems to have been obscured in this production.'

Christopher Milton flashed her a frank, confiding smile. 'I agree, Mrs Crichton-Smith, but Goldsmith was writing for his time. This is 1975, we can't just do a production as if nothing has changed since the play was written. And, anyway, this is not *She Stoops to Conquer*, this is a new musical. What we're trying to do, and I think our writer, Kevin McMahon, would agree with me here,' he added, as if to impress the image of a big-happy-family, all-working-towards-the-same-end company, 'is to create an original show. I mean, entertainment is variety. Your husband wouldn't think much of you if you produced the same meal for him every night—however good it was.'

His middle-class half-joke produced the right middle-class half-laugh and Charles was once again impressed with Christopher Milton's ability to adapt to any audience and say the right things. It was not an intellectual gift; he probably did not have the intelligence or knowledge to argue the merits of the piece on a literary level; it was just an instinct that never failed.

Miss Thompson, the secretary, next introduced a question from: 'Mr Henry Oxenford, one of our keenest members, who's interested in all things theatrical.' Mr Oxenford, one of the bow-tied types who hang about amateur dramatic societies, content to be precious rather than queer, stood up and put his well-rehearsed enquiry, 'I would like to know whether you, as a performer, be it as Tony Lumpkin or Lionel Wilkins, find the danger that a part tends to take over your private life and you become like that person?'

Christopher Milton laughed boyishly. 'You mean when I'm working on the television series, do I go around trying to con money off everyone I meet?'

'Well, not exactly.'

'Oh, I beg yours.' The Lionel Wilkins line was, as ever, perfectly delivered and got its laugh. Charles watched Christopher Milton's eyes and saw him decide to continue in the Wilkins voice and prolong the misunderstanding. 'Oh, I see what you mean—do I go up to people in the street and say, Look'ere, I've got this great project. Wouldn't you like to buy shares in the first motel on the

moon? Not only do you get the normal dividends, but you
also get a free weekend every year once the motel is
completed. Now the shares aren't yet officially on the
market, but I can let you have some at a price which. . . .'
And he was away, re-creating the plot of a recent episode
of *Straight Up, Guv*. The Friends of the Palace Theatre
loved it.

As he drew to the end of his routine, before Miss
Thompson could introduce Mrs Horton who had been
waving her arm like a schoolgirl know-all between each
question, he glanced at his watch. 'Oh, look at the time.
I'm afraid we've gone on much longer than we intended.
We've still got a lot of work to do on this show—oh, you
may have liked it, but there are a good few things to be
altered yet—so we must draw it to a close there.'

The Friends of the Palace Theatre started to leave
through the stalls. An autograph cluster gathered round
the star. The other members of the cast, who hadn't got
much of a look-in on the discussion, trickled back
through the curtains. Mark Spelthorne dawdled, seeing if
there were any fans of *The Fighter Pilots* on the
autograph trail. When it became apparent there weren't,
he vanished smartly.

Christopher Milton finished the signings and waved
cheerily from the stage until the last Friend had gone out
of the doors at the back of the stalls. When he turned his
face was instantly twisted with rage. 'Cows! Stupid,
bloody cows!' He pushed through the curtains, shouting
imperiously, 'Wally! Dickie! Come on, we've got to get
this script altered, even if we have to work all bloody
night.'

As Charles waited to hear the inevitable news that
there would be a rehearsal call at ten the following
morning, he began to understand the personality-splitting
pressure of a public image.

Gerald Venables was sitting waiting in his car, a Mercedes
280 SL, with the lights doused, by the stage door. He had
the collar of his raincoat turned up and was slumped
against the window in an attitude cribbed from some

B-movie. He was trying so hard to be inconspicuous that Charles saw him instantly. 'Hello.'

'Ssh. Get in.' The passenger door was slipped open. Charles climbed in clumsily. 'So, what gives?' Gerald hissed, his eyes scanning the empty road ahead.

'Just been a bit of a dust-up, boss,' Charles hissed back.

Gerald didn't realise he was being sent up, but ran out of slang. 'What? You mean a fight?'

'Too right, boss.'

'Irons?'

'I beg your pardon.'

'Irons—you know, guns. God, don't you watch any television?'

'Not much.'

'Well, give us the dirt. Who swung a bunch of fives at whom?' The grammatical resolution of the question rather weakened its underworld flavour.

Charles gave a quick account of the scene in the green room and the solicitor nodded knowingly. 'So you reckon this McMahon could be our cookie?'

'Our saboteur, the man devoted to the destruction of the show ...?'

'Yes.'

'I don't know. Certainly he hates Christopher Milton. If anything were to happen to the star tonight, I would have no doubt about who to look for. But I don't think Kevin can have been responsible for the other accidents, not the first two, anyway.'

'Why not?'

'Because why should he? When the pianist was shot at, Kevin didn't know what was going to happen to his script, rehearsals had hardly started. I reckon at that stage he must have been full of excitement, you know, his first West End show and all that.'

'But it can't have taken long for him to realise the way things were going.'

'Yes, I suppose he could have built up a sufficient head of resentment by the time Everard Austick met with his accident.'

'Yes, surely, and—'

'There's another snag, Gerald. Kevin's resentment is completely against Christopher Milton. Sniping at these minor figures may be bad for the show, but it doesn't hurt the star much. Christopher Milton doesn't care who his supporting cast are, so long as they don't argue with him or do anything better than he does. If Kevin McMahon did want to get at anyone he'd go straight for the one who was bugging him—and, with the star out of the way, there might be a chance that his musical could survive in another production.'

'Yes. So we've got to look for someone else as the mastermind behind the whole sequence of crimes.'

'If there is a sequence, Gerald, if there are any crimes. So far the only evidence I have of misdoing is what happened at the King's Theatre. I know someone tampered with the rope holding those flats up. All the others could be genuine accidents. In fact, the thing at the King's may have a perfectly legitimate explanation.'

'I don't know, Charles. I still have the feeling that they're all linked and that something funny's going on.'

There was a silence. 'Hmm. Yes, I can feel a sort of foreboding too, but I don't know why.'

As he spoke, light spilled across the road from the stage door. Christopher Milton, Dickie Peck, Wally Wilson and the show's musical director, Pete Masters, came out, escorted by Milton's driver, who smartly moved forward to the parked Corniche and opened the doors. They all got in. 'Let's follow them,' whispered Charles, more to satisfy Gerald's love of the dramatic than anything else.

They let the Rolls disappear at the junction on to the main road, confident that Leeds' central one-way system would make it difficult to lose their quarry, and started up in pursuit.

Gerald's 'Follow that car' routine was as exaggerated as his 'I am waiting unobtrusively' one, involving many sudden swivels of the head and bursts of squealing acceleration alternating with dawdling so slowly that it drew hoots of annoyance from other road-users. But the inhabitants of the Rolls did not appear to notice them.

There were none of the sudden right-angled swerves up side-roads beloved of gangsters in movies. They drove sedately round the one-way system and into Neville Street, where they swung off the main road and came to rest at the entrance of the Dragonara Hotel. Gerald, who hadn't been expecting the stop, overshot, screeched to a halt and reversed to a spying position, flashed at by the righteous headlights of other drivers in the one-way street.

The party disembarking from the Corniche still did not take any notice of their pursuers. The four of them walked straight into the foyer and the driver slid the car away to the hotel car park.

'Well . . .' said Gerald.

'Well, I guess we've found out where he's staying.'

'Yes. Yes, we have.'

'I could have asked him and saved us the trouble.'

'Yes, but at least this way we can tell if he's lying.'

'What on earth do you mean? Why should he lie about staying in the newest, poshest hotel in Leeds?'

'I don't know.' They both felt very foolish.

'By the way, Gerald, why aren't you staying at the Dragonara? I thought that was your usual style.'

'I didn't know it existed. Polly, my secretary, booked me into the Queen's. More traditional, I think . . . I'm only here for the one night. I suppose I could try and get transferred, see if there's a room here.'

'What good would that do?'

'Well, then I'd be in the hotel, I could spy, I. . . .'

'What are we spying on? What do we want to find out?'

'I don't know.'

'All we want to do is see that Kevin McMahon doesn't get a chance to have a go at Christopher Milton.'

'Yes.'

'And since he's got Dickie Peck and his driver in the hotel there with him, I think we're superfluous.'

'So what should we do?'

'Go to our several beds,' said Charles, with mingled desire and depression at the thought of his.

'All right. I suppose we'd better. Mind you, we're going to feel pretty silly in the morning if we hear that Christopher Milton's been murdered.'

They needn't have worried. Christopher Milton survived the night unharmed. But Kevin McMahon was found beaten up in the car park by the bus station.

Eight...

CHARLES DIDN'T HEAR about the new accident until he reached the theatre for rehearsal. A silent breakfast with Ruth had been followed by a silent lift in her Renault 5L to the city centre. She started work at nine, so he had time to kill. They parted in silence and he wandered off in the direction of the Dragonara for no apparent reason.

To occupy his mind with trivialities, he pretended he was trailing the man in front of him. The head he followed was completely bald with enormous ears like the handles of a loving cup. Charles varied his pace, playing a game with himself, committing details to memory, checking the time. At five to nine the man went in the front entrance of the Dragonara and the game was over.

Charles looked round for someone else to use as a dummy and then felt a wave of hopelessness. What was the point of playing at detectives when his performance was so abysmal on the occasions that required real detective abilities?

The 'what was the point?' gloom deepened to embrace his emotional life too. Another night of angry sex with Ruth had depressed him. What was the point of it? He had left Frances to get away from the ties and twists of a 'relationship', hoping to find some kind of freedom. And he had accepted the limitations which the emotional free-lance shares with all other free-lances—delays between engagements and sudden terminations of contracts. But it wasn't just that. Casual sex didn't give him enough and anything deeper soon got claustrophobic. If he was going to go through all the hard work of making something work, he might just as well try again with Frances. At least he had got a start there.

But Frances had got a boy friend. So the rumour went, and he had no cause to disbelieve it. And that seemed to change it all. It twisted his emotional outlook. He would not admit to himself that he was prey to so simple an emotion as jealousy, but the fact that Frances was not floating unattached in the background made any other relationship more threatening, as if now he was really looking for something lasting. Which he wasn't....Oh, hell, why couldn't he just think of Ruth as a nice time in Leeds, all to be over and forgotten in a week? But guilt crept in, and though he was conscious of his depression over-dramatising everything, he was unable to get out of the pointless spiral of his thoughts.

He quickly got news of Kevin's accident when he arrived at the theatre. The police were there. They had taken over one of the dressing-rooms, where they were questioning members of the cast. There were constant assurances that no one in the company was suspected, but certain facts had to be established—who Kevin was, where he was staying and so on.

The details of the beating spread quickly. Kevin was in the Infirmary though he was not seriously hurt. Apparently he had spent the evening drinking, moving on to a small club when the pubs closed. He had been kicked out of there at about two, and wandered round for some time—he couldn't remember how long—and then been jumped by someone who punched him in the face, kicked him about the rest of his body, left him unconscious and stole his wallet. The police regarded it as a simple mugging and were looking for someone local.

They did hear about the altercation between Kevin and Dickie Peck and when the agent arrived with his protégée at ten-thirty, he was questioned. But it transpired that the two of them, along with Wally Wilson and Pete Masters, the young musical director, had been up most of the night working on a new number to replace *Liberty Hall*. They had mutually dependent alibis.

That was a blow to Charles' simple reading of the situation. He had leapt to the conclusion that Dickie Peck must have got at Kevin, continuing the scene that had started in the green room. And if there had only been Christopher Milton and Wally Wilson to corroborate Dickie's alibi, he would still have believed it. But if Pete, the M.D., also vouched for him, that changed things. He was not one on the star's immediate entourage and the most unlikely person to submit to intimidation. So maybe it was just an attack by a mugger unknown. But it did seem too much of a coincidence.

And if it was a coincidence, it was a very happy one for Christopher Milton. There was no dissenting voice when he announced that *Liberty Hall* was to be dropped and that the whole day until the evening performance would be spent rehearsing the new number which had been written overnight.

He was very ebullient and cheerful. He made no pretence now that David Meldrum was directing the show and leapt around the stage telling everyone what to do and demonstrating. He showed no fatigue after the long night and was supremely creative. His enthusiasm for the new song was infectious and they all worked hard to give it life.

Pete Masters, the M.D., had written a simple but catchy tune and was very pleased with himself. Wally Wilson had written the lyric and when Christopher Milton first sang it through with the piano, Charles could feel the gyrations of Oliver Goldsmith in his grave accelerate yet again.

> *When you're out of the fiddle*
> *And you're trying to pull a con*
> *And the cops come in the middle*
> *Of the trick you're trying on,*
> *Then all you've gotta do*
> *Is just give a little pause,*
> *Give a little smile*
> *And come back with 'I Beg Yours?'*

Not 'I beg to differ' or 'I beg to remain...'
Not 'I beg your pardon', but an easier refrain,
Not 'I've lost my bottle' and not 'I've lost my drawers'—
The answer's very simple—
All you say is 'I Beg Yours?'

When you're selling some jew'l'ry
And the jew'l'ry don't exist
And the victim of your fool'ry.
(Who you thought was very...drunk)
Turns out to be a cop
And says he'll bring down the laws,
Don't lose your cool,
But come back with 'I Beg Yours?'

Not 'I beg to differ' or... and so on through four more verses of variable scansion and anachronism. Christopher Milton ended the song with a flourish and Charles couldn't help joining in the applause that followed it. He was once again struck by how good Christopher Milton was. The applause was not sycophancy; it was the genuine praise of professionals.

But in spite of the performance, the song was hopelessly wrong for the show. Charles knew it and felt he had to say something. He was just assembling a tactful objection when Mark Spelthorne came in with his own drawling complaint. Typically, it was completely selfish. 'But we can't really have that number there, Christopher. I mean, that would make it three solos for you in a row. Surely, it would be better for the balance of the show if we had an ensemble number at this point.' (What he really meant was, 'I had a lot to do in *Liberty Hall*. Now I've lost a number.')

Christopher Milton did not snap back at Mark. He didn't bother when Dickie Peck was present to do it for him. 'That's nonsense,' barked the agent. 'The audience will have come here to see Christopher Milton and the more of him they see, the happier they'll be.'

'There is such a thing as over-exposure,' Mark Spelthorne observed in a voice that wouldn't remain as cool as he wanted it.

'Something you're never going to have to worry about, sonny,' Dickie flashed back. 'No, it's a great number. Really good. Just done overnight, you know—' (appealing for admiration from the company. Charles' admiration conformed with Dr Johnson's comment about a dog walking on its hinder legs—'It is not well done, but you are surprised to find it done at all.') '—No, I think this is going to be the number of the show. Make a great single too. I don't see actually why it shouldn't be the title of the show. *I Beg Yours?*, I mean it's catchy and it's—'

'All the publicity's already gone out,' David Meldrum interposed, thus at least killing that ridiculous idea. But Charles still thought someone ought to question the suitability of the number for a show which, in spite of major surgery and transplants, was still set in the eighteenth century and was about Tony Lumpkin rather than Lionel Wilkins. It would stick out like go-go dancers in the middle of the Ring Cycle.

He cleared his throat to remonstrate, but fortunately Winifred Tuke anticipated him. 'We can't have this song.'

'Why not?' asked Dickie Peck aggressively, pausing with match held up to a new cigar.

'Well, honestly, darling, I mean, I know we're not doing *She Stoops* . . . straight, but this does make nonsense of it.' It was daring and impressive and she should have left it at that. Instead she went on, getting more actressy and vague. 'I mean, the whole thing about this play is that it's Town life versus Country and we're already losing that by playing Tony London, but if we start putting in bits from other shows then—'

'It isn't a bit from another show,' said Christopher Milton softly.

'Not exactly, darling, but this song is absolutely based on that divine character you play in the telly, and I mean it just isn't Tony Lumpkin . . . is it?'

Her ginny voice faltered as he gazed at her coldly. The tableau was held in silence for a full minute. Then

Christopher Milton turned to David Meldrum and said, unfairly, 'Come on, we should be rehearsing if we're to get this number in by tonight.'

'And are we?'

'Yes, we bloody are. For Christ's sake assert your authority.' Which was rich, coming from the person who had done most to undermine it.

I Beg Yours? was in the show on the Tuesday night. It was under-rehearsed and a little untidy, but the audience loved it. Once again, Christopher Milton's instinct seemed to have been vindicated. The reaction to the rest of the show was mixed, but they latched on to that number.

Ruth was out front. Charles had given her a ticket, though after their silent parting in the morning he wasn't certain that she'd come. However, there she was at the stage door after the show. When he saw her, he felt an awful sense of shame. It was not exactly that he was ashamed of her, but he felt wrong with her. He tried to hurry her away, but Michael Peyton called out to him just as they were leaving, 'Hey, everyone's going out for a curry. You want to come?'

Charles started to refuse, but Ruth chipped in and said she hadn't eaten and would love to go.

He hated the meal, because he hated being thought of in conjunction with Ruth. He knew how cruel it was to resent someone's company in that way and the knowledge only made him feel guiltier. Ruth, on the other hand, enjoyed herself. Surprisingly, Christopher Milton and Dickie Peck had joined the party, the star having decided to be one of the boys for a night, and he chatted up Ruth shamelessly. She luxuriated in this and Charles, embarrassed by her naïve questions and provincial tastes, was annoyed to find that he felt jealous too. To be jealous about a woman whom he was embarrassed to be with, it all got far too complicated to cope with. He drank heavily and wished Frances were there.

Ruth was drunk too and drove back unsteadily,

chattering about Christopher Milton, to the grim inevitability of bed.

There was a small paragraph in the *Yorkshire Post* on the Wednesday morning, which mentioned the mugging of Kevin McMahon. From the management's point of view, it could have been worse. It didn't make a big issue of the incident and, on the bonus side, it was a free advertisement for the show.

The morning's rehearsal schedule was more work on *I Beg Yours?*, which didn't involve Charles, so, hoping to shrug off the depression engendered by the scene with Ruth, he set off for the home of Kevin McMahon's parents. Remembering a mention of Meanwood in their conversation in the pub, he easily found the right McMahons in the phone book and rang them to check that Kevin was out of the Infirmary.

He travelled by bus. The pebble-dash semi had a two-tone doorbell.

Mrs McMahon was small and sixtyish, with fuzzy white hair. She went on about how nice it was for one of Kevin's friends from the play to come along and treated Charles like one of her son's school friends. She also muttered regretfully about this terrible thing happening to Kevin on the night of his great triumph.

'You enjoyed the show on Monday?'

'Oh, we thought it was grand. That Christopher Milton, he's lovely, isn't he? I bet he's one of those who's just the same offstage as he is on. No *side*, if you know what I mean, isn't that right?'

Charles replied appropriately, making a mental note that Kevin was beyond the age for confiding in his parents.

The writer was in his childhood bedroom and seemed to have grown younger to match his surroundings. There was a poster of the Leeds United team of 1961. Uneven piles of magazines and carefully dusted Airfix aeroplane models suggested that his mother had kept his room 'just as he liked it' for whenever he decided he needed the comfort of home. But this could hardly have been the return she had hoped for.

Kevin's eyes were nearly closed by puffy blue lids. Face criss-crossed with strips of plaster and open scratches. His right hand was bandaged in gauze and one finger stiffened with the square outline of a splint. No doubt the covers hid comparable injuries on the rest of his body.

'How're you doing?'

'Not too bad, Charles. It's good of you to come.' He was subdued and formally polite, as if his surroundings brought back years of being taught good manners.

'No problem. I wasn't called for rehearsal this morning. They're doing the new—something that doesn't involve me.'

Kevin showed no interest in what was happening to the show. There was a silence.

'Was it very bad?'

'I don't know. I think I was more or less anaesthetised by alcohol at the time it happened.' Charles chuckled encouragingly. 'And when I came round, the hangover was so bad I hardly noticed my injuries. It's only today I'm really beginning to feel it.'

'Sorry.'

'Not too bad. Just very stiff all over. As if every bone in my body has been pulled out of its socket and reassembled by an enthusiastic amateur.'

'Hmm. Do you mind talking about it?'

'No, but there's nothing to say.'

'Why not?'

'I was so honked I can't remember anything. There was one bloke, that's all I know. And no, I didn't get a look at him. The police have asked me all this.'

'You couldn't even say whether he was old or young?'

'No. Why do you ask that?'

Charles decided honesty might elicit the best response. 'I was wondering if it was Dickie Peck who got at you.'

'Dickie Peck? Why?' The question was dully asked; there was no animation.

'Well, you had that fight earlier in the evening....'

'Yes.' He sounded very tired. 'Look, Charles, I was

mugged. It's not nice, but it happens. I have no reason to believe it was anyone I know who did it. My only comfort is that it was hardly worth his while. I'd drunk away practically all the money I had, so all he got was a couple of credit cards.'

'Did he say anything to you, or just hit?'

'Just hit.' Kevin winced at the recollection.

'Surely the average mugger starts by asking for the goods and then comes in with the heavy stuff when you refuse.'

'I don't know.' The intonation was meant to end the conversation, but Charles had to continue. 'Kevin, Dickie Peck protects Christopher Milton like a eunuch in a harem. If anyone argues with his blue-eyed boy, he stops them. And I don't think he's too fussy about his methods. He used to be a boxer and, as we saw the other night, he's still pretty tough.'

'I was mugged,' said Kevin doggedly.

'You're not holding out on me? There is nothing to make you think it could have been Dickie?'

'I am not holding out on you. There is nothing to make me think it could have been Dickie,' came the repetition on a monotone.

Charles sighed. 'Okay. Thanks. Well, I expect you'll soon feel better. What'll you do—come down and join us in Bristol?'

'No, I don't think I'll bother.'

'What?'

'I think I'll follow your earlier advice—take the money and run. What was it you said—that I must think of it as a grant to buy time to go off and write what I really want to? That's what I'll do. There's no point in going on banging my head against a brick wall.'

'Or having your head banged against a brick wall.' But Kevin did not rise to the bait. Whoever it was had got at him had achieved the objective of the Christopher Milton/Dickie Peck camp. There would be no more interference in *Lumpkin!* by the writer of *Liberty Hall.*

He managed to get a word with Pete Masters, the musical

director, during a break in the morning rehearsal. 'Good number, that *I Beg Yours?*' he offered. Compliment is always conducive to confidence.

Pete, however, showed discrimination. 'It's all right. Rather cobbled together. I don't really think it's that great. Lyric could do with a bit of polishing. The basic tune's okay, but it needs a proper arrangement. I'll do it as soon as I get time.'

'Still, the product of one night. A whole song. Did you find it hard?'

'What, doing it in the time? Not really. Did lots of revue at—university and got used to knocking up stuff quickly.'

'People who hesitate before they say "university" either went to somewhere so unmentionably awful that they're afraid of shocking people or went to Oxbridge and are afraid of being thought toffee-nosed.'

Pete's boyish face broke into a smile. Charles' guess had been right. 'Cambridge, actually.'

'Ah, the Footlights.'

'Exactly. By the way, you're right, people do get a bit shirty if you talk about it. Especially in the music business.'

'Did you read music?'

'Yes.'

'So this is slumming for you.'

Again the tone had been right. Pete laughed. 'You could say that.' As he relaxed, his nondescript working-with-musicians voice gave way to his natural public school accent.

'Tell me, when you wrote that new song, did you actually stay up all night?'

'Oh yes.'

'In the Dragonara?'

'In Christopher Milton's suite, yes.'

'And you all worked on it, him and you and Wally and Dickie Peck?'

'Yes. Well, we talked it through first and then Wally and I went down to the ballroom, which was the only place where there was a piano. I think Christopher Milton and Dickie may have got some sleep while we did that.'

'Or I suppose they could have gone out. . . .'

Pete treated the idea as a joke rather than as grounds for suspicion, which was just as well. 'What, in Leeds? There's nothing to do here during the day-time, leave alone at night.'

Charles chuckled 'So how long did it take you and Wally actually to write the number?'

'I don't know exactly. I suppose we went down to the piano about two-thirty and maybe finished about five.'

So it was possible that Dickie Peck could have left the hotel to get Kevin McMahon. If, of course, he knew where to find him. Which was unlikely. But possible. The case seemed full of things that were possible, but not likely.

Charles wandered aimlessly around Leeds, trying to work it out, just to get one line of logic through all the strange events of the past few weeks. But it seemed as impossible to impose a pattern as it was to work out the geography of Leeds town centre. After half an hour of circling round identical pedestrian shopping precincts, he went into a little restaurant called 'The Kitchen' in Albion Street.

Over the Dish of the Day and a glass of red wine, he got out a notebook and pencil bought for the purpose in a W. H. Smith's he'd passed three times in the last half hour. James Milne, whom he'd met in Edinburgh over the Mariello murder the previous summer, had taught him the advantages of writing things down to clarify thoughts.

Three headings—'Incident', 'Suspect' and 'Motive'. In the first column—'Pianist shot at', 'Everard Austick pushed downstairs', 'Flats allowed to fall' and 'Kevin McMahon beaten up'. He filled in a question mark after the first two, thought for a moment, and put one after the third. He started on 'Suspects'. Dickie Peck and Christopher Milton's driver for the second two 'Incidents' and question marks for the first two. 'Motive' offered 'Protection of C.M., seeing that he gets his own way', again only for the second two. More question marks.

If only he could get some line which linked the first two victims with the later ones. He'd asked Michael Peyton about any altercations between the star and the pianist or Everard and received the information that, in the first case, the two didn't even meet at rehearsal, and in the second, an atmosphere of great cordiality had been maintained. So, unless there were some unknown link in the past, the motive for the first two attacks couldn't be the same as for the subsequent ones. Oh dear. He had another glass of wine.

In one respect at least the attack on Kevin McMahon had changed the situation. It had been publicly re-cognised as a crime by the cast, the police, the Press. That meant that any subsequent incidents might be related by people other than Charles and Gerald Venables. The criminal, if criminal there were, would have to be more careful in future.

Having come to this conclusion, Charles looked at his watch. Five to two. God. There was a two-thirty matinée on Wednesday and if he hadn't signed in at the theatre by the 'half', there'd be trouble.

In fact, there was trouble, but not the sort he feared. It was gastric trouble, and it only affected one member of the cast, Winifred Tuke.

Very interesting. If the pattern of accidents Charles suspected did exist, and if the motivation he had assumed were correct, then it was natural that Winifred Tuke should be the next victim. Since her clash with Christopher Milton over *I Beg Yours?*, she had made no secret of her feelings and, being a theatrical lady, she made no attempt to make her umbrage subtle. Gastric trouble also fitted. After the dramatic fate of Kevin, the criminal was bound to keep a low profile. Winifred Tuke had to be punished for opposing the will of Christopher Milton, but it couldn't be anything too serious, just an embarrassing indisposition which would put her out of action while the new number was rehearsed and became an established part of the show.

She had started to feel queasy at the end of the matinée, and only just managed to get through the last number. She did not appear for the curtain call. The company manager questioned her in her dressing-room and gathered, not so much from her genteel explanations as from her constant departures to the Ladies, that she was suffering from acute diarrhoea. She was sent back to her digs in a taxi, moaning imprecations against the previous night's curry, and her under-rehearsed understudy took over for the evening performance.

Charles was not convinced about the curry. For a start, he would have expected food poisoning to manifest itself more quickly, and also it seemed strange that Winifred Tuke should be the only one affected by it. The meal had been one of those occasions when everyone ordered something different and had a bit of everything.

But nobody else seemed worried and certainly no one talked of links between the incident and Kevin's mugging. It seemed strange to Charles that in a large company of actors, who are the most superstitious of people, no one had spoken of bad luck or a jinx on the show. Perhaps he was too close to it. If it hadn't been for his unconventional recruitment, he probably wouldn't have found anything odd himself.

But at least this could be investigated. If Winifred Tuke had been slipped something, the chances were it had happened in the theatre. So, in the dead time between the matinée and evening performance, Charles took a look around.

The silence of empty dressing-rooms is almost tangible. He could feel the great pull of sentimentality which has led song-writers to maunder on about the smell of grease-paint, the limpness of unoccupied costumes, the wilting flowers, the yellowing telegrams of congratulation and all that yucky show business rubbish. Distant sounds from the stage, where the indefatigable Spike and his crew were going through yet another flying rehearsal, served only to intensify the silence.

Fortunately, Winifred's hasty exit had left her dressing-room unlocked. Inside it was almost depressingly tidy. A neat plastic sandwich-box of make-up, a box of tissues and a Jean Plaidy paperback were the only signs of occupation. Someone with Winifred's experience of touring didn't bother to settle in for just a week.

What Charles was looking for was not in sight, but it didn't take him long to find it. His clue came from the smell on Winifred Tuke's breath during rehearsals and, more particularly, performances. It was in the bottom of the wardrobe, hidden, in a pathetic attempt at gentility, behind a pair of boots. The middle-aged actress's little helper, a bottle of Gordon's gin.

The investigation was an amateur detective's dream. It was so easy Charles almost felt guilty for the glow of satisfaction it gave him. He opened the bottle and sniffed. Gin all right. He took a cautious sip and immediately felt suspicious. It wasn't the taste, but the consistency, the slight greasiness the drink left on his lips.

He poured a little into a glass and his suspicions were confirmed. Though it didn't show through the dark green of the Gordon's bottle, in the plain glass it was clear that the liquid had separated into two layers. Both were transparent, but the one that floated on top was viscous and left a slight slime round the glass. He dabbed at it and put his finger to his tongue. Yes, he wouldn't forget that almost tasteless taste in a hurry. It was his prep school matron's infallible cure for constipated boys—liquid paraffin.

He was excited by the discovery, but controlled his emotions while he washed up the glass. The slime clung on stubbornly and he had to wipe at it with a tissue.

A doubt struck him. If he had discovered the doctoring of the drink so easily, why hadn't Winifred noticed it? But the concealment of the gin bottle in the wardrobe answered that. If she kept her drinking a secret (or at least thought she did), then probably she would only whip the bottle out for a hasty gulp and pop it straight back to its hiding place. And if she'd been drinking during the show, she would probably put the greasy taste down to make-up on her lips.

Charles felt breathlessly excited. Here at last was evidence. Though every other apparent crime could have been an accident or the work of a vindictive outsider, the bottle was evidence of deliberate misdoing, committed within the company.

He had to keep it. In a case where facts were so thin on the ground he couldn't afford not to. Winifred Tuke was far too genteel to report its disappearance and, considering the bottle's contents, he was doing her a favour by removing it.

His holdall was in the green room, so he set off there, gin bottle in hand. Stealth was unnecessary; nobody would be in for the evening performance for at least an hour. He trod heavily on the stairs, awaking the echoes of the old building. He pushed open the green room door with a flourish and realised that he had forgotten the stage staff.

Spike and some others were slumped on sofas, reading newspapers. Charles made an involuntary movement to hide the bottle.

He needn't have worried. Spike was the only one who stirred. He looked up mildly and said, 'Didn't think that was your usual tipple, Charles.'

Charles made some half-joke about ringing the changes, put the bottle in his holdall and went out to the pub. He gave himself a mental rap over the knuckles for bad security. It didn't really matter, because only Spike had seen him. But it could have been someone else and it was his job as investigator to keep a low profile.

Still, he'd got the bottle. Perhaps a diarrhoea weapon lacked the glamour of a murder weapon, but it certainly warranted a large whisky.

Now all he had to do was find a link between the bottle and his chief suspect. Difficult. Dickie Peck had returned to London that afternoon. Never mind, the investigation would keep until he rejoined the company.

Significantly, with the agent away, in spite of occasional flashes of temper from Christopher Milton, there were no more incidents while *Lumpkin!* was in Leeds.

PART 3

Bristol

Nine...

CHARLES WAS GLAD to get to Bristol. He hadn't enjoyed the previous few days. Investigations apart, Leeds had ended in scenes of cynical recrimination with Ruth. After a final fierce coupling on the Sunday morning and a silent drive to the station, he had had a long slow journey to King's Cross for her unspoken accusation to fester in his mind. He couldn't just laugh it off. As many times before, he cried out for the ability to say, that was good while it lasted, or that didn't work, oh well, time to move on. But he was bad at the sort of insouciance that should have accompanied his style of sex life. Feelings kept snagging, he kept feeling sorry for people, kept feeling he was using them. And, as always, lacking the self-righteousness necessary for anger, he ended up feeling self-disgust.

A half-day in London hadn't helped his mood. The bed-sitter in Hereford Road had not got less depressing in his absence. With the change in the weather it was as cold as a morgue when he opened the door. Nor did Sunday papers he'd bought offer any cheer. Bombs in London restaurants and the continuing apparent hopelessness of the Herrema siege led to fears of the imminent collapse of society, that terrible plunging feeling that tomorrow everything will stop and animal chaos will reign.

He rang his wife Frances in an attempt to shift the mood. But her phone just rang and rang and he stood, his finger dented by the twopence in the coin-box and his mind drifting, trying to remember what she had said in their last conversation about this new man she was seeing, forming silly fantasies of her with the new man, even of her upstairs in their bed with him, hearing the phone and saying, 'Shall we answer it?' and him saying, 'No'. It was stupid, childish; it was as if he were again a sixteen-year-old, his stomach churning as he asked his first girl out to the pictures. And this was Frances, for God's sake, Frances whom he knew so well, who was so ordinary he had left her. But his feelings swirled around, unanchored. He put the phone down.

Back in his room (the telephone was outside on the landing) he had turned immediately to the obvious solace, a half-full (or, in his current mood, half-empty) bottle of Bell's. He drank with the kamikaze spirit of self-pity, sadly identifying with Everard Austick.

So Bristol, by comparison, was pleasant. He got a lift down on the Monday morning with a couple of the dancers who lived in Notting Hill and, apart from the fact of being in company, the staged sparkle of their camp chatter put him in a good mood. Then there was where he was staying. Julian Paddon, an actor friend from way back, was a member of the resident company at the Old Vic and had issued an immediate invitation when he heard *Lumpkin!* was coming to Bristol. His wife Helen was charming and had the enormous advantage after Ruth that Charles didn't fancy her at all (and even if he had, she was eight months pregnant and thus satisfactorily *hors de combat*).

Julian, whose nesting instinct, always strong, had been intensified by regular employment and the prospect of an addition to his family, had rented a flat in a Victorian house in Clifton and Charles was made to feel genuinely welcome.

Lumpkin! too responded to the new town. The day's break after the heavy rehearsal schedule in Leeds meant that everyone came to it with renewed vigour. The makeshift musical arrangement for *I Beg Yours?* had been improved and expanded by Leon Schultz, an American arranger flown over at enormous expense by an edgy management. The song was greatly enhanced and on the first night in Bristol it stopped the show. Once again Christopher Milton's theatrical instinct had been vindicated. The management was so pleased with the song that they asked Schultz to do new arrangements for all other numbers in the show. It would mean a lot more rehearsal, but in the new mood of confidence no one complained.

Away from the gloom of Leeds, Charles found it difficult to believe in thoughts of sabotage. The long sequence of crimes he had rationalised became unreal, another part of the general confusion over the show and Ruth which Leeds had meant for him. When he unpacked at Julian's flat, he had to look closely at the Gordon's gin bottle to convince himself that anything criminal had ever happened.

Part of his relaxation was due to Dickie Peck's absence. His suspicions had now homed in firmly and until the agent rejoined the company, he did not fear further incidents. What he should do when another occurred was something he tried not to think about.

Anyway, rehearsals kept him busy. Desmond Porton from Amulet Productions was to come and see the show on the Thursday and give the final all-clear for the scheduled first night at the King's Theatre on Thursday, November 27th. That gave a sense of urgency and a healthy edge of determination to everyone in the show.

The first two nights made Charles begin to think he was, for possibly the first time in his life, about to be connected with a success. Apart from reflections on the irony of a fate which withheld major triumph from shows he had cared about in favour of the commercial banality of *Lumpkin!*, it was a pleasant feeling.

He was sitting in the pub during the Tuesday performance (having dutifully checked in for the 'half' and let the stage manager know where he'd be) when the girl approached him. Her pale blue eyes had the unfocused stare of contact lenses, but there was nothing vague about her manner. 'Are you in *Lumpkin!*?' she asked, the directness of the question emphasised by an American accent.

'Fame at last,' he replied with irony. 'Yes, I am.'

'Good, I thought I recognised you. I saw the show last night.'

'Ah.' Charles left the pause for comment on his performance which no actor can resist.

But the girl didn't pick up the cue. 'My name's Suzanne Horst,' she said. 'I'm a free-lance journalist.'

He emitted another 'Ah', again succumbing to an actor's instinctive reaction that the girl wanted to write something about him.

She soon put him right on that. 'I'm trying to make contact with Christopher Milton.'

Of course. He blushed for having suspected anything else, and let out another multi-purpose 'Ah'.

'Would you introduce me to him?'

'Well. . . .' This was rather difficult. The past month with Christopher Milton had revealed to Charles how carefully the star's contact with the press and media was regulated by his agent. To introduce an unexpected journalist could be a serious breach of professional etiquette. 'I think probably the best thing you could do would be to make contact with his agent. It's Dickie Peck of Creative Artists.'

'I don't want to mess with agents. Anyway, I'm here in Bristol. What's the point of contacting a guy in London about someone who's only a hundred yards away at this moment?'

There wasn't a great deal of logic about it, but that was the way stars worked, Charles explained.

She was not put down. 'Yes, I know that's the correct way to go about things, but I don't want to go the correct way. I want to go the way that'll get me the interviews I'm after.'

'Well, I don't know what to suggest.' Charles felt churlish, but thought he was probably doing the right thing. 'What are these interviews you are after?'

'One's for radio. Only got Radio Brighton interested at the moment, but I'm sure I'll be able to get it on one of the networks. That's only secondary, anyway. The main thing I want him for is an article I'm doing on the nature of stardom. Want to know what makes him tick, you know.'

'Who's that for?'

'Don't know who I'll offer it to yet. *Cosmopolitan*, maybe.'

'It hasn't been commissioned?'

'No, but I'll sell it all right.' Whatever Miss Horst lacked, it was not confidence.

In fact she didn't lack much. Certainly not looks. Her shoulder-length hair was that streaky yellow which might be the natural result of sun on brown hair or the unnatural result of hairdressers on any colour. Her belted Burberry formalised but did not disguise her lithe figure, and though her overpowering confidence might be a slight deterrent, the general effect was distinctly tangible. 'Can I get you a drink?'

'Thank you. A vodka and tonic, please.' The barman eyed Charles knowingly as he supplied the drink. Suzanne didn't seem to notice. 'Are you sure you can't introduce me?'

'Honestly, it is difficult. You know, people like Christopher Milton have to guard their privacy very carefully. I'm afraid they tend to be a bit resistant to journalists.'

'But, look, I'm not going to do a big exposé or anything. It'll be an appreciative piece. I mean, I'm a fan.'

'I don't think that's really the point. It's rather difficult to get near him.'

'But you see him at rehearsal, don't you?'

'Well, yes, but—'

'Then you could ask him if he'd be prepared to do an interview with me.'

Her persistence didn't make it easy. Charles cringed with embarrassment at the thought of putting the girl's request to Christopher Milton. It was difficult to explain to someone outside the closely defined relationship that exists between actors in a working context. 'Look, I'm sorry, I really don't think I can.'

'Why not? You do know him, don't you?'

'Yes, I do, but—'

'Well then,' she said, as if that concluded the syllogism.

'Yes.' Under normal circumstances he would have

given a categorical 'No', but under normal circumstances the people who made this kind of request didn't look like Suzanne Horst. He said something about seeing if he had a chance to raise the matter at rehearsal (which he had no intention of doing) and asked the girl how much journalism she had done.

'Oh, quite a lot in the States. I got a degree in it, but the scene over there isn't very interesting, so I decided to check it out over here.'

'What, you've given yourself a sort of time limit to see if you can make it?'

'Oh, I'll make it.'

Charles was beginning to find this self-conviction a little wearying, so he brought in a damper. 'Yes, unfortunately it's a bad time to get started in that sort of area at the moment. Journalism's getting more and more of a closed shop. It's like acting, getting increasingly difficult to make the initial break into the business.'

'Don't worry,' said Suzanne, as though explaining to a child, 'People with talent always get through.'

He couldn't think of anything to say after that.

But Suzanne suddenly got an idea. 'Hey, you could actually be quite useful on this stardom article.'

'In what way?'

'Well, you could give me a bit of background on Christopher Milton. After all, you're working with him.'

Charles was hesitant, but overruled. She had whipped out a new shorthand notebook and a freshly-sharpened pencil and was poised in the attitude of someone who had taken a degree in journalism. The question came out formal and rehearsed. 'Tell me, as an actor, what do you think it is that makes some people stars?'

'And some dreary old hacks like me? Hmmm. Well now—' dropping into an American accent—'what is a star? What is it that picks out one from the myriad throng of the moderately talented and gives him that magic name? What is it that sets one talent glowing in the limelight, that scatters the moondust of stardom on that one chosen head? Is it of the earth or is it made in heaven? Perhaps in that Great Casting Agency in the Sky, there sits the one Eternal Agent who—'

'Look, are you taking the rise out of me?'

He lapsed back into his normal voice. 'No, sorry. I was just getting my bearings. Stardom? I don't know really. In the sort of theatre I normally do it's rarely an issue.

'But I suppose, if I had to give an opinion. . . . Well, talent certainly, that must be there. Not necessarily a great deal of it, nor anything very versatile. In fact, there should be no versatility. The star must always be recognisable—if he puts on voices, he must put them on almost badly, so that everyone knows it's him. That's talent. Okay. What else? Dedication certainly, the conviction that what he does is more important than anything else in the world.'

'Isn't that likely to lead to selfishness?' Suzanne interposed with studied professionalism.

'Inevitably. Bound to. Hence, presumably, all the stories that one hears of stars hating competition and being temperamental and slamming dressing-room doors and that sort of thing.'

He realised that it could get a little awkward if Suzanne asked him to relate his last observation to the star of *Lumpkin!*, and hurried on before she had the chance. 'I think there's also something about the way the entertainment industry works, certainly for actors. Being an actor is, potentially, the most passive function on earth. Most actors are completely dependent on directors, because it's directors who control the jobs. Some manage to assert themselves by deep commitment to their work, or by directing or writing or devising shows. Some do it by political affiliations—starting street theatres, work-shop communes, even—in cases of extreme lunacy—joining the Workers' Revolutionary Party. Some do it by forming their own companies, that kind of thing. But what I'm getting at is that, given this lack of autonomy, when an actor becomes very much in demand, as a star might be, he wants to dictate his own terms. It's years of frustration at living on someone else's terms. It's also a self-preservation thing—once someone's got to the top, he tries to do everything to ensure that he stays there, and that may involve being careful about the people he works with, seeing that none of them are too good. I mean, often when you see a show with one big star name above the title and the rest of the cast nonentities, it's not just because the star's fee has exhausted the budget, it's also that he shows up in such mediocre company. The Whale among Sprats syndrome.

'Then there's management, which is very important. Choosing work, not doing anything that's beneath the star's dignity, or anything in which he's not going to shine. Can't take a risk, everything that is done has to be right, even at the expense of turning work down. For that reason you often find that a real star won't do anyone a favour, won't step in if someone's ill. It's not just bloody-mindedness, it's self-preservation. When someone's at the top, there are any number of people sniping, ready to read the signs of a decline, so it never does to be too available.'

'Do you think a star has *magic?*' asked Suzanne, with awe-struck italics.

'I don't know. I—'

'Oh, Mr Paris, there you are.' Gwyneth of the stage management stood before him, her customary calm ruffled by anxiety. 'You should have been back in the theatre half an hour ago.'

On the Wednesday morning they were rehearsing the first act finale, *Ooh, What a Turn-up*, which had been rearranged by Leon Schultz. Pete Masters, the M.D., was not in the best of moods. Having seen his own arrangements thrown out of the window, he found it galling to have to teach the new ones to the impassive band. The musicians had long since lost any spark of interest that they may have had for the show and sat mentally sorting out their VAT returns, eyes occasionally straying to their watches to see if the rehearsal would spread over into another session at M.U. rates. Christopher Milton was onstage directing, while David Meldrum sat at the back of the stalls reading *The Stage*.

The rehearsal had reached an impasse. Leon Schultz's new arrangement introduced a short violin figure which bridged from the verse into the chorus and there was no dancing to cover it. The cast tried freezing for the relevant three seconds, but that lost the pace of the number. A couple of the dancers improvised a little jig, which looked alien and messy. There was a long pause while Christopher Milton stood centre stage, the ominous faraway expression in his eyes.

Suddenly he was galvanised into action. 'Where's the sodding choreographer?'

'She wasn't called for this rehearsal,' said the musical director smugly, 'following assurances that the new arrangements would not involve any major changes in the choreography.'

Christopher Milton seemed not to hear the dig. It was as if his mind could only focus slowly. 'Then what can we do?' He enunciated the words very clearly and without emotion.

'No idea.' Pete Masters shrugged. 'Unless we cut the meaningless little bit of schmaltz altogether.' His tone was calculated to provoke, but produced no reaction. Emboldened, he pressed on: 'Or go back to the original arrangements, which were quite as good and a darned sight less fussy.'

'What, your arrangements?' Christopher Milton asked slowly.

'Yes.'

'Your sodding arrangements.' The build to anger was slow, but now it had started it built to a frightening intensity. 'Your little tuppenny-ha'penny amateur tea-shop quartet arrangements. This is the bloody professional theatre, sonny, not some half-baked student revue. Your arrangements! This isn't Penge Amateur Operatic Society, you know.'

Pete Masters' face had gone very red, but he fought to keep his voice calm and give a dignified reply. 'There's no need for you to speak to me like that. You may prefer the new arrangements to mine, but there's no need to be offensive about it.'

'Oh, I'm sorry, was I being offensive?' The last word was pronounced with savage mimicry that exactly echoed Pete's public school tone. 'How foolish of me. I had forgotten that I was speaking to someone who has a

degree in music and therefore knows everything about the
subject. What a silly-billy I am.'

The impersonation was funny and, though Charles
cringed in the wings and the musicians continued to stare
impassively, it did produce an unidentified laugh from
somewhere up in the flies where the stage crew were
invisibly watching the proceedings. It gave Christopher
Milton a stimulus and he continued to vent his lacerating
irony on Pete.

Eventually the M.D. struck back. Still he tried to
sound in control, but his wavering voice let him down.
'Listen, if you're going to speak to me like that, I'm going.'

'Go. See if anyone cares. Just don't think you can treat
me like that. You've got to get it straight, boy, what
matters in this show. You don't. You go, there are a
hundred second-rate musicians can take over tomorrow. I
go, there just isn't a show. Get your priorities right, boy.'

Pete Masters mouthed, but couldn't produce any
words. He did the only possible thing in the circumstances
and walked off stage. The musicians looked at their
watches with satisfaction. A row like this made it almost
certain that they'd go into another session. The atmosphere in the theatre was heavy with embarrassment.

It blew over. Of course it blew over. That sort of row
can't go on for long. The pressures of keeping the show
going don't allow it. Pete and Christopher Milton were
working together again within a quarter of an hour, with
neither apologising or commenting on the scene. All the
same, Charles Paris was relieved that Dickie Peck had not
been present to witness the latest challenge to his protégé.

It wasn't just the clash at rehearsals that morning, but
something changed the company mood on the Wednesday afternoon. Perhaps it was a small and silent house at
the matinée. Perhaps it was Desmond Porton's impend-
ing visit and the fear of having the show assessed. Or
perhaps it was The Cold.

Actors, whose working tools are their voices, are
naturally terrified of colds, sort throats, 'flus and other
infections which threaten their precious vocal cords. They

all have their own favourite remedies and preventative methods when germs are in the air, or, in some cases, even when they aren't. Large doses of Vitamin C are swallowed, dissolved or crunched. (So are most other vitamins of the alphabet, with a kind of pagan awe.) Strange elixirs of lemon and honey (with bizarre variations involving onions) are poured down tender throats. Aspirin, codeine, paracetamol, Anadin, Veganin and others are swilled down, discussed and compared as connoisseurs speak of malt whiskies. Names of doctors who can 'do wonders for throats' (as well as others who deal with backs and nervous twinges) are exchanged like rare stamps. It is all taken very seriously.

When a show involves singing, the panic and precautions are doubled. Vocal sprays are brought into play. Little tins and envelopes of pills are ostentatiously produced and their various merits extolled. Some favour Nigroids, small pills which 'blow your head off, dear, but really do wonders for my cords'; others will not stir without 'The Fisherman's Friend'—'quite strong, darling, but they really relax the throat'; there are Friar's Balsam, Vocalzones, Sanderson's Throat Specific and a whole gallery of other patent medicines available, all of which have their staunch adherents.

The Cold started with one of the dancers, who had difficulty in preventing his sneeze during the matinée. Then Mark Spelthorne, quick to seize any opportunity for self-dramatisation, thought he might have one of his throats coming on. During the evening performance many of the cast were walking round backstage massaging their throats, talking in whispers ('conserving the voice, dear—may have a touch of 'flu coming on') and generally putting on expressions of private suffering which they had learnt when rehearsing Chekhov. It helped to make the atmosphere around *Lumpkin!* suddenly spiky.

Charles just made it to the pub as time was being called after a sedate Bristol house had given its qualified support to the evening performance. He was the only one of the company who went. Most went straight home to nurse themselves in anticipation of The Cold.

He managed to get in an order for a pint of bitter (performing always made him thirsty) and was letting the first mouthful wash down when the girl came up to him. The American voice twanged. 'Did you ask him?'

'Who? What?' He pretended innocence, but knew full well what she meant.

'Christopher Milton. You were going to ask him about the interview.'

'Oh yes, of course. I hadn't forgotten. Trouble is, today was very busy, what with the two shows. And we were rehearsing some new arrangements this morning.' It sounded pretty feeble.

But she didn't seem to notice. 'Never mind. You'll do it sometime.' Surprisingly benign. He'd expected her to tear him apart for his omission. 'Some time,' she repeated and he realised that she was drunk.

'Can I get you a drink?'

'Haven't they closed?'

'Nooo. Never. Barman. What is it, Suzanne?'

'Vodka tonic.'

'One of those, please.'

She took the drink and gulped it down like water. She stood close to him and swayed so that they almost touched. 'How'd the show go?'

'Not world-shattering.'

"Smy birthday today.'

'Ah.'

'Had a few drinks to celebrate. Alone in a foreign country.'

'Ah.'

She leant against him. 'Give me a birthday kiss. Back in the States I never go without a birthday kiss.'

He kissed her dryly on the lips as if she were a child, but he felt uncomfortably aware of how unchildlike she was. Her breasts exercised a magnetic attraction as she swayed towards him. He drained his beer. 'Well, better be off. They'll be turfing us out shortly.'

'You going to see me home?' she asked kookily. Miss

Suzanne Horst with a few drinks inside her was a very different proposition from the hyper-efficient lady who was about to set British journalism afire.

'Is it far?'

'Not far. Staying at a hotel.'

'Ah.' Charles found he said a lot of 'Ahs' in conversation with Suzanne. Because he couldn't think of anything else to say.

They hadn't got far from the pub when she stopped and rolled round into his arms. 'Kiss me properly,' she mumbled. Light filtered across the road from the lamp over the stage door.

He held her warm and cosy in his arms. He didn't kiss her. Thoughts moved slowly but with great clarity through his mind. The girl was drunk. He was nearly fifty. He should keep away from women; it always hurt one way or the other. The silent resentment of Ruth was too recent a memory. And before that there had been Anna in Edinburgh. And others. A wave of tiredness swept over him at the eternal predictability of lust.

He felt a shock of depression, as if the pavement in front of him had suddenly fallen away. What was the point of anything? Women could alleviate the awareness of the approach of death, but they could not delay it. He was cold, cold as though someone was walking over his grave. The intensity and speed of the emotion frightened him. Age, it must be age, time trickling away. He thought of Frances and wanted her comforting touch.

The girl in his arms was still, half dozing. He took her elbow and detached her from him. 'Come on. I'll get you back to your hotel.' Gently.

At that moment he heard the clunk of the stage door closing and looked across to see Pete Masters emerge with a brief-case under his arm. The M.D. didn't see him, but started to cross the road, going away from him.

The Mini must have been parked near by, but Charles wasn't aware of it until it flashed past. He turned sharply, seemed dumb for a moment, then found his voice, too late, to shout, 'Look out!'

Pete Masters half-turned as the wing of the Mini

caught him. He was spun round on his feet and flung sprawling against a parked car. From there he slid down to lie still in the road. The Mini turned right at the end of the street and disappeared.

Ten...

AND DICKIE PECK had not been in Bristol at the time of the accident. Charles tried to reason round it, but the fact was incontrovertible. According to Christopher Milton, the agent was not expected to come and see *Lumpkin!* again until Brighton. In case that information wasn't reliable, Charles went to the extreme of phoning Creative Artists to check it. He used a disguised voice and pretended to be a policeman investigating the accident to Pete Masters. It was a risky expedient, one that had turned sour on him before, but he couldn't think of another. As soon as he put the phone down, he realised that if Dickie Peck had anything to hide, he was now going to be a hundred times more careful. And he could well have been lying about his movements anyway.

All the same, Charles had already started to remove the agent from the front rank of his suspicions. Though he might be involved, might be directing operations, Dickie Peck wasn't the one to do the heavy stuff. The more Charles thought about it, the more incongruous it became—a successful agent, with a lot of artists on his books, going round running people over and slipping them liquid paraffin? No. What was needed was a logical reappraisal of the situation.

He sat in Julian Paddon's sitting-room on a bright autumn day and once again wrote down James Milne's headings, 'Incident', 'Suspect' and 'Motive'. He only filled in the middle column. Three names—Dickie Peck, Christopher Milton and Christopher Milton's driver.

Then, as if imposing logic by committing conjecture to paper, he wrote another heading, 'Reasons for Innocence'. Against Dickie Peck's name he filled in, 'Not on scene of last incident (i.e. in London)—position to keep up—discovery would ruin career'. Against Christopher Milton—'Last point above to nth degree—v. concerned with public image—could not afford the risk of personal action'. Against the driver he put a neat dash, then changed his mind and wrote, 'The only question is who he's taking orders from—D.P. or C.M.—or is he acting off his own bat?'

Written down it looked convincing, Charles felt a satisfaction akin to completing *The Times* crossword. He couldn't imagine why he hadn't thought of the driver before. Very distinctly he remembered the first time he had seen the man, advancing threateningly towards the crowd of boys who mobbed Christopher Milton outside the Welsh Dragon Club. He remembered how the driver had been halted by a gesture and how he had hovered protectively until the star wanted to leave. Like a bodyguard. It was quite logical that Christopher Milton should have a bodyguard. People in the public eye are instant targets for freaks and lunatics. And in a way everything untoward that had happened on the show could be put down to an exaggerated interpretation of a bodyguard's rôle. Whether the man interpreted it that way for himself or at someone else's suggestion was a detail which could wait until there was some actual evidence of guilt.

In Charles' new mood of logical confidence he felt sure that proof would not be difficult to find now that he had a definite quarry. He took his sheet of paper with the winning formula on it and burnt it carefully in the grate of the fireplace, pulverising the black ash until it could yield nothing to forensic science. Even as he did so, a sneaking suspicion that he concentrated too much on the irrelevancies of detection started to bore a tiny hole in his shell of confidence.

'Charles, what the hell's going on?'

'What do you mean, Gerald?'

'Well, there's a little piece in the *Evening Standard* about this M.D. being run over.'

'Ah.'

'It also mentions Kevin being mugged in Leeds. No comment, just a juxtaposition of the two facts. It's worse than if they actually said it's a bad luck show.'

'Oh, come on. If someone's run over, it doesn't necessarily mean there's anything odd. Accidents do happen.'

'But don't you think this is another in the series?'

'As a matter of fact I do, but nobody else does. There's no talk about it in the company, beyond the sort of relish actors always have for dramatic situations.'

'Have the Press made much of it down there?'

'Not a lot. Small report, just the facts. M.D. of *Lumpkin!*—hit and run driver in stolen car—details of injuries, that's all."

'What were his injuries?'

'Mainly bruising. I think he may also have broken his patella.'

'His what?'

'Kneecap to you.'

'And he's out of the show?'

'Certainly for a bit. Leon Schultz has taken over as M.D.'

'Has he?' Gerald sounded gratified. 'Ah, well, it's an ill wind. Good. I always said they should have got a big name from the start rather than that boy. It'll bump the budget up a bit.'

The welfare of the show seemed to be Gerald's only concern. So long as his investment was protected, nothing else mattered. Charles felt bitter, particularly as his friend continued, 'But look, do keep a watchful eye on Christopher Milton. If he gets clobbered, the show really is a non-starter.'

'And if anyone else gets clobbered, it doesn't matter?'

'Well, yes, it does, of course, because it's very bad publicity for the show, but it's Christopher Milton who's the important one. And they must be aiming for him eventually, otherwise there's no point in all this, is there?'

'That's not the way I see it. I don't think I should worry about Christopher Milton; I should be protecting everyone else in the show.'

'What do you mean?'

'Nothing. I can't explain it now. Suffice to say that my view of the case has changed since we last spoke.'

'Oh. But do you know who's doing it all?'

'Yes. I think I do.'

'Well, get him arrested and stop him.'

'I haven't got any evidence yet.'

'Then get some.'

'I will.'

Charles felt furiously angry when he put the phone down. The whole thing was getting out of proportion. The protection of Christopher Milton must continue, whoever got hurt on the way. It was hearing such blinkered lack of consideration from Gerald that made him so cross. The world, even his friends, would forgive anything done in the name of Christopher Milton. Gerald had asked for evidence and an arrest and he'd get them, though they might not be what he expected. Charles felt a wave of anger against the whole star set-up, the charming public persona that needed the support of thuggery to survive. Whether or not Christopher Milton was directly involved in the crimes, the rottenness and meanness of what had been going on should be exposed to the public. From now on Charles wasn't working for Gerald Venables representing Arthur Balcombe. He was working for himself.

After the Thursday show, he dressed carefully for his midnight jaunt. As an actor, he knew how much the right costume could help in a difficult rôle, and the rôle in which he had cast himself was a very difficult one.

He wore a pair of his own black trousers and a black sweater borrowed from Julian (in what he hoped was a casual manner). He had bought a pair of plimsolls in Woolworth's and, since Woolworth's don't sell ready-dirtied plimsolls for house-breakers, he had shabbied them up with earth from Julian's garden. Other investments were a balaclava helmet and a pencil torch. He knew the preparations were over-elaborate, but they took his mind off what he had to do.

With the balaclava on, he looked like a very young photograph of himself as Second Sentry in *Coriolanus* ('Leaden production'—*Richmond and Twickenham Times*). Without it, he looked a cross between himself as Lightborn in a modern dress *Edward II* ('Flamboyantly sinister'—*Birmingham Evening Mail*) and as Jimmy Porter in *Look Back in Anger* ('Ill-considered'—*Luton Evening Post*). He crept down the stairs to the front door and realised he was using the walk he'd perfected for *Rookery Nook* ('Uneven'—*Jewish Telegraph*).

Unfortunately he met Julian coming in. 'Where are you going dressed like that, Charles? You look as if you're about to commit a burglary.'

That didn't help.

Residents of the Holiday Inn in Bristol park their cars in the adjacent multi-storey car park. It was a simple matter to walk in. He found Christopher Milton's distinctive Rolls on the first level without any problem.

And his luck held. The Corniche was unlocked. He slipped in by the passenger door and closed it quickly to douse the interior light. He reached to get the torch out of his pocket, but his hand was shaking too much. He closed his eyes and practised rib-reserve breathing, trying to keep the thought of what he was doing at bay. But a schoolboy fear of being found out remained. He wished he could remember some of the relaxation exercises various experimental directors had tried to put him through. None came.

Still, the deep breathing helped. He opened his eyes and, very slowly, like a man under water, he got out the torch and switched it on.

The glove pocket opened easily. A tin of boiled sweets came first into the light. He prised it open and found nothing but the sugary debris that should have been there. Next a large stiff envelope. He felt inside. The shiny surface of photographs. He pulled one out and shone the

torch on it. Christopher Milton grinned cheerily at him.
Fan photographs. The sight of the familiar face brought
on another pang of guilt. At the same moment he noticed
that his thumb had left a perfect print on the photograph.
The light caught it on the shiny surface. That was one that
the police wouldn't need powder to spot. He wiped at it
roughly, but seemed only to add more prints. He shoved
the photograph back into the envelope and replaced it.

Sweat prickled on his hands and he thought he'd done
enough. His grandiose schemes for following the raid on
the car with a search of the driver's hotel bedroom were
evaporating fast.

Finish the glove pocket and go. He ran his fingers
along the angle at the back and felt some small bead-like
objects under his finger-nails. He picked one out, held it
between thumb and fore-finger and turned the light on it.

And at that moment his whole attitude to what he was
doing changed. What he held was a small-waisted piece of
lead. The shape was unmistakable. It was an airgun pellet.
Just the sort of airgun pellet which had hit *Lumpkin!*'s
first rehearsal pianist in the hand on the second day of
rehearsal. It was evidence.

He grabbed three or four more of the slugs and put
them in his pocket. His panic had changed to surging
confidence. He reached forward for one more sweep into
the glove pocket and his hand closed round the firm
outline of a small bottle. Hardly daring to hope, he drew it
out and flashed the torch on it. LIQUID PARAFFIN (Liquid
Paraffin BP). The bottle was half-empty. He could not
believe his good fortune.

There was a noise of a door banging. He turned.
Someone was coming from the direction of the hotel. A
guest going to another car. He'd wait for them to drive off
and then beat a hasty retreat. He shrank down into the
leather seat and slipped the balaclava helmet over his
head. He pulled it round to cover his face.

The silence was unnaturally long. No slam of a car
door, no choking of an engine. He began to think that the
visitor must have gone out down the ramp and slowly
eased himself up to look.

At that moment there was a click of the door opening and he felt light through the latticed wool of the balaclava. He was face to face with Christopher Milton's driver, who was leaning forward to get into the car.

The man's eyes bulged as he saw the intruder and in shock he jerked his head back sharply. There was a loud crack which shook the car and he slid gracefully from view.

Charles, his mind full of ugly pugilistic visions, edged slowly across to the driver's seat and looked down over the edge.

The driver lay neatly on the ground with his eyes closed. He was out cold. Charles got out of the car, shut the door to put the light out and turned his torch on the body on the ground.

There was no blood. Regular breathing. Strong heart-beat. Strong pulse. Probably just concussion. He loosened the man's tie and put a cushion from the back of the car under his head.

Then, with the precious pellets and bottle in his pocket, Charles crept down the stairs out of the garage. As he emerged into the street, he removed the balaclava.

There was a phone-box opposite. It seemed a natural conclusion to the dream-like flow of luck which had characterised the previous half-hour. Charles dialled 999 and asked for the ambulance service in his own voice before thinking to disguise it. When he was connected, he had a moment's agonising decision choosing a voice. Northern Irish seemed the most natural for this sort of thing, but it might be unduly alarmist in a bomb-conscious Britain. The voice that came to hand was American-Italian. Sounding like something out of *The Godfather*, he said, 'Could you send an ambulance to the big car park beside the Holiday Inn.' He was tempted to say, 'There's a stiff there', but made do with, 'There's somebody injured'.

'What's happened to them?' asked the voice and it was only by putting the phone down that Charles could prevent himself from saying, 'Someone made him an offer he couldn't refuse'.

He hung about until he saw the ambulance safely arrived, and then went briskly back to Julian's place, using the walk he'd developed when playing a gangster in *Guys and Dolls* ('This guy didn't like it and nor did the doll he was with'—*Bolton Evening News*).

Eleven...

CHARLES WOKE IN an excellent mood. The events of the previous night were very clear to him. It was as if he had found the instant cure-all he had always dreamed must exist somewhere. All his problems had been resolved at once. He now had evidence of the wrong-doing of the driver and just to make his job easier, the driver himself was temporarily removed from the scene. There was still the minor question of what he should do about it—confront the villain and threaten police proceedings, go direct to the police or send them an anonymous deposition advising investigation—but that would keep. The warm completed-*Times*-crossword sensation had developed into an even better feeling, as if his solution to the puzzle had won a prize.

Helen Paddon cooked him an enormous breakfast, which he consumed with that relish which only a fulfilled mind can give. She was pleased to have something to do. The last heavy weeks of pregnancy were dragging interminably.

He finished breakfast about nine and took the unusual expedient of ringing Gerald at home. After pleasantries and must-see-you-soons from Kate Venables, the solicitor came on the line. 'What gives?' he asked in his B-film gangster style.

'It's sorted out.'

'Really?'

'Uhuh.' Charles found himself slipping into the same idiom.

'You know who's been doing it all?'

'I know and I've got evidence.'

'Who?' The curiosity was immediate and childlike.

'Never mind.' Charles was deliberately circumspect and infuriating. 'Suffice to say that I'll see nothing else happens to threaten the show, at least from the point of view of crime or sabotage. If it fails on artistic grounds, I'm afraid I can't be held responsible.'

'Is that all you're going to tell me?'

'Yes.'

'Damn your eyes.' Charles chuckled. 'But you're sure that Christopher Milton is in no danger?'

'I don't think he ever has been in any danger from anyone but himself.' On that cryptic note he put the phone down, knowing exactly the expression he had left on Gerald's face.

There was a ten-thirty call for the entire company to hear what Desmond Porton of Amulet Productions had thought of *Lumpkin!* and what changes he had ordered before the show could come into London. Charles ambled through the streets of Bristol towards the theatre, his mood matched by the bright November sun. The people of the city bustled about their business and he felt a universal benevolence towards them. His route went past the Holiday Inn and he could hardly repress a smile at the memory of what had happened the night before. It was strange. He felt no guilt, no fear that the driver might have been seriously hurt. That would have spoiled the rounded perfection of the crime's solution.

The people of Bristol looked much healthier than those of Leeds. His mind propounded some vague theory about the freedom of living near the sea as against the claustrophobia of a land-locked city, but it was let down when the sun went in. Anyway, the people didn't look that different. In fact, there was a man on the opposite side of the street who looked exactly like the bald man with big ears whom he'd idly followed in Leeds. He kicked himself for once again trying to impose theories on everything. Why could he never just accept the continuous variety of life without trying to force events into generalisations?

There was a lot of tension at the theatre. The entire company sat in the stalls, exchanging irrelevant chatter or coughing with self-pity to show that they'd got The Cold. There were three chairs on the stage and, as Charles slumped into a stalls seat, they were filled by the company manager, David Meldrum and Christopher Milton.

David Meldrum stood up first as if he were the director and clapped his hands to draw attention. The chatter and coughing faded untidily. 'Well, as you all know, we had a distinguished visitor in our audience last night, Desmond Porton of Amulet, who, you don't need reminding, are putting up a lot of the money for this show. So for that reason, if no other, we should listen with interest to his comments and maybe make certain changes accordingly.'

'Otherwise the show will never make it to London,' added the company manager cynically.

'Yes.' David Meldrum paused, having lost his thread. 'Um, well, first let me give you the good news. He liked a lot of the show a lot and he said there is no question of the London opening being delayed. So it's all systems go for November 27th, folks!' The slang bonhomie of the last sentence did not suit the prissy voice in which it was said.

'And now the bad news. . . .' For this line he dropped into a cod German accent which suited him even less. 'We were up quite a lot of the night with Desmond Porton going through the script and there are quite a lot of changes that we're going to have to make. Now you probably all realise that over the past few weeks the show has been getting longer and longer. Our actual playing time is now three hours and eight minutes. Add two intervals at fifteen minutes each and that's well over three and a half.'

A derisive clap greeted this earnestly presented calculation. David Meldrum appeared not to hear it and went on. 'So that means cuts, quite a lot of cuts. We can reduce the intervals to one, which would give us a bit of time, and the King's Theatre management won't mind that because it saves on bar staff. But we've still got half an hour to come out of the show. Now some of it we can lose by just shortening a few of the numbers, cutting a verse and chorus here and there. We can probably pick up ten

minutes that way. But otherwise we're going to have to
lose whole numbers and take considerable cuts in some of
the dialogue scenes.

'Now I'm sorry. I know you've all put a lot of work into
this show and I know whatever cuts we make are going to
mean big disappointments for individuals among you.
But Amulet Productions are footing most of the wage bill
and so, as I say, we have to listen carefully to their views.
And after all, we have a common aim. All of us here, and
Amulet, we all just want the show to be a success, don't
we?'

The conclusion of the speech was delivered like Henry
V's 'Cry God for Harry, England and St George!' but was
not greeted with the shouts of enthusiasm which follow
Shakespeare's line in every production. There was an
apathetic silence punctuated by small coughs until one of
the dancers drawled, 'All right, tell us what's left, dear.'

David Meldrum reached round for his script, opened it
and was about to speak when Christopher Milton rose
and said, 'There was another point that Desmond made,
and that was that a lot of the show lacked animation. Not
enough action, not enough laughs. So as well as these
cuts, there will be a certain amount of rewriting of the
script, which Wally Wilson will be doing. It's all too
sedate at the moment, like some bloody eighteenth-
century play.'

'But it is a bloody eighteenth-century play.' Charles
kept the thought to himself and nobody else murmured.
They were all resigned—indeed, when they thought about
it, amazed that the major reshaping of the show hadn't
come earlier. They sat in silence and waited to hear the
worst.

David Meldrum went through the cuts slowly and
deliberately. They were predictable. Oliver Goldsmith,
whose revolutions in his grave must by this time have been
violent enough to put him into orbit, was left with almost
nothing of his original play. The trouble with most
musicals based on other works is that the songs are not
used to advance the action. A musical number is merely a
break in the continuity and, when it's over, you're four

minutes further into the show and only two lines further into the plot. Carl Anthony and Micky Gorton's songs, written with an eye to the Top Ten and continuing profitable appearances on LPs, were particularly susceptible to this criticism. But because the songs were the set-pieces and the items on which most rehearsal time and money had been spent, they had to survive at the expense of the text. Charles, who remembered Goldsmith's play well from his own Cardiff production, saw the plot vanishing twist by twist, as one of the most beautiful and simple comic mechanisms in English literature was dismantled and reassembled without many of its working parts.

But the cuts were selective. It was clear that Christopher Milton had been up through the night with David Meldrum and Desmond Porton, watching each projected excision with a careful eye. Tony Lumpkin's part came through the massacre almost unscathed. One rather dull number was cut completely and a verse and chorus came out of another. And that was it. While all the other characters had their parts decimated.

The one who suffered most was the one who Goldsmith, in his innocence, had intended to be the hero, Young Marlow. Cut after cut shredded Mark Spelthorne's part, until he had about half the lines he had started the day with.

For some time he took it pretty well, but when the proposal to cut his second act love duet with Lizzie Dark was put forward, his reserve broke. 'But that's nonsense,' he croaked. (He was suffering from The Cold and was determined that no one should miss the fact.)

'Sorry?' asked David Meldrum mildly, but the word was swamped by a sharp 'What?' from Christopher Milton.

'Well, putting on one side for a moment the fact that the play no longer has a plot, if you cut the love duet, there is absolutely no romantic content from beginning to end.'

'Yes, there is. There's my song to Betty Bouncer.'

'But that song has nothing to do with the plot. Betty Bouncer doesn't even appear in the original play.'

'Sod the original play! We aren't doing the original play.'

'You can say that again. We're doing a shapeless hotch-potch whose only *raison d'être* is as a massive trip for your over-inflated ego.'

'Oh, I see. You think I'm doing all this work just to give myself cheap thrills.'

'I can't see any other reason for you to bugger up a plot that's survived intact for two hundred years. Let's face it, it doesn't matter to you what the show is. We might as well be performing a musical of the telephone directory for all you care. Just so long as you've got all the lines and all the jokes and all the songs. Good God, you just don't know what theatre's about.'

'I don't?' Christopher Milton's voice was ominously quiet. 'Then please tell me, since I am so ill-informed on the matter, what the theatre is about.'

'It's about team-work, ensemble acting, people working together to produce a good show—'

'Bullshit! It's about getting audiences and keeping in work. You go off and do your shows, your 'ensemble theatre' and you'll get nobody coming to see them. People want to see stars, not bloody ensembles. I'm the reason that they'll come and see this show and don't you kid yourself otherwise. Let me tell you, none of you would be in line for a long run in the West End if this show hadn't got my name above the title. So don't you start whining about your precious lines, Mark Spelthorne. Just think yourself lucky you've got a job. You're not going to find them so easy to come by now they've dropped that bloody awful *Fighter Pilots*.'

That got Mark on the raw. 'How the hell did you know that?'

'I have contacts, sonny. As a matter of fact, the Head of London Weekend Television was down this week trying to get me to do a series for them. He told me.'

'It's not definite yet,' said Mark defensively. 'They're still considering it. The producer told me.'

'It's definite. The producer just hasn't got the guts to tell you the truth. No, your brief taste of telly stardom is over and let me tell you, no one's too anxious to pick up the failed star of a failed series that didn't make the ratings. So if I were you, I'd keep very quiet in this show, take what you're given and start writing round the reps.'

The public savagery of the attack gave Mark no alternative but to leave the theatre, which he did. What made the denunciation so cruel was that it was true. Mark Spelthorne had risen to public notice in advance of his talents on the strength of one series and without it he wasn't much of a prospect.

As usual the star continued addressing his audience as if nothing had happened. 'Now the next scene we come to is the Chase, the *Lead 'em Astray* sequence. I don't think we need cuts in this one. In fact I don't think we've begun to develop that scene yet. I discussed this with Desmond Porton and he agrees that we can add a whole lot more business and make it a really funny slapstick sequence. We're going to do it in a sort of silent film style, with a lot more special effects. And I think we can pep up the choreography a bit in that scene. Really get the girls jumping about.'

'You try jumping about in eighteenth-century costume,' complained an anonymous female dancer's voice.

Christopher Milton did not object to the interruption; he continued as if it were part of his own train of thought. 'Yes, we've got to change the girls' costumes there. Get more of an up-to-date feel. Like go-go dancers. Really get the audience going.'

'Why not have them topless?' drawled one of the dancing queens.

'Yes, we could—no.' His objection was, needless to say, not on grounds of anachronism. 'We've got to think of the family audience. I think this Chase Scene can be terrific. Wally Wilson's working on it now and we can make it into something really exciting. Going to mean a lot more work, but it will be worth while. Oh, that reminds me, we're going to need flying equipment for it....

'What?' asked David Meldrum weakly.

'Flying equipment for the Chase Scene. I'm going to be flown in on a Kirby wire. Have we got the stuff?'

'No, I don't think so. We'd have to get it from London.'

'Well, get it. Who organises that?'

'I suppose the stage manager.'

'Is he about?'

'Yes, I think he's backstage somewhere.'

'Then get him to organise that straight away. I want to start rehearsing with it as soon as possible.' As if under hypnosis, the man whose title was 'director' wandered offstage to find Spike. 'Now, in that sequence, we're also going to be making a lot more use of the trap-doors and doubles for me.... Okay. It's going to make that bit longer, but I think it'll give the show a great lift towards the end....'

Charles' part was so small that, short of cutting it completely (and in the current climate, that did not seem impossible), the management could not do it much harm. As it was he lost four lines and left the theatre for the pub feeling that it could have been a lot worse. Just as he went through the stage door, he met Spike coming in. 'Oh, they were looking for you. Something about a Kirby wire.'

Spike's *papier mâché* face crumpled into a sardonic grin. 'They found me. Yes, so now his Lordship wants to fly as well as everything else. It'll be walking on the water next.'

Charles chuckled. 'I wonder if he's always been like this.'

'What do you mean?'

'Always ordering everyone about. I mean, he couldn't have done it when he started in the business, could he?'

'With him anything's possible.'

'Where did he start? Any idea?'

'Came out of stage school, didn't he? Suppose he went straight into rep.'

'You've met lots of people in the business, Spike. Ever come across anyone who knew him before he became the big star?'

There was a pause. 'I don't know. I'm trying to think.' Spike wrinkled his face; when the acne scars were in shadow, he looked almost babylike. 'There was an actor I

once met who I think had been with him a long time back.
Now what was his name ...? Seddon ... Madden, something like that. Paddon, that's right.'

'Not Julian Paddon?'

'Yes, I think that was the name. Why, do you know
him?'

'I'm only staying with him here in Bristol.'

Mark Spelthorne was sitting in the corner of the pub. It
was only eleven-thirty and there weren't many people
about. Charles felt he couldn't ignore him. 'Can I get you
a drink?'

'Brandy, please. Medicinal. For the cold.' He looked
frail. His nose was comically red, the lines of his face were
deeply etched and for the first time Charles realised that
the hair was dyed. Mark Spelthorne was older than the
parts he played. As Christopher Milton had said,
overcoming the current setback in his career wouldn't be
easy.

Charles ordered the brandy and a pint of bitter for
himself. That meant he was in a good mood. He drank
Scotch when he was drinking to change his mood or delay
a bad one and beer when he wanted to enjoy the one he
was in.

'Cheers.' They drank. Charles felt he could not ignore
what had happened. 'Sorry about all that this morning.
Must've been pretty nasty for you.'

'Not the most pleasant few minutes of my life.'

'That I believe. Still, he says things like that in the heat
of the moment. He doesn't mean them.'

'Oh, he means them.'

Though he agreed, Charles didn't think he should say
so. He made do with a grunt.

'Yes, he means them, Charles, and what's more, he's
right.'

'What do you mean?'

'They aren't going to do any more *Fighter Pilots*.'

'Well, so what? Something else will come up.'

'You reckon? No, he's right about that too. They
launched that series to see if it caught on. If it had, I'd have

been made, got star billing from now on. But now it's failed, nobody'll touch me.'

'Oh, come on. You'll keep in work.'

'Work, yes. Supports, but not star billing. My career's ruined.'

Charles tried to remember if he'd ever thought like that. So far as he could recollect, his aim in the theatre had always been for variety rather than stardom. Still, it obviously mattered to Mark. He tried another optimistic tack. 'But there'll be other chances. I mean, you made this pilot for your own radio show . . .?'

'Yes. They don't want it. It's been heard and they don't want to make a series.'

'Ah, ah well.' Charles searched through his store of comforts for such situations and could only come up with cliché. 'Never mind, one door closes, another one opens.' It was patently untrue. In his own experience life's doors worked like linked traffic lights—one closed and all the others closed just before you got to them.

Mark treated the platitude to the contemptuous grunt it deserved. 'My God, he's such a sod. I feel so angry, just so angry.'

'Yes,' Charles said, inadequately soothing.

'And the world loves him. *Lovable* Christopher Milton. Every time he's mentioned in the Press, there it is, lovable Christopher Milton. Doesn't it make you puke? If only his precious public could see him as he was this morning, could see all the meanness that goes to make up his lovability. My God, do people have to be that unpleasant to appear lovable?'

'He works hard at his public image. It's all very calculated.'

'Yes, calculated and untrue. He has no integrity, his whole life is a masquerade.' Mark Spelthorne spoke from a position of extreme righteousness, as if his own life had never been sullied by a shadow of affection. 'You know, I think I'd give anything to expose him, show him to the public for what he really is—a mean-minded, egotistical, insensitive bastard.'

'But talented.'

'Oh yes. Talented.' Even in the violence of his anger Mark could not deny the facts.

Charles thought a lot about what Mark had said. Because possibly he held in his hands the power to expose the star. If the series of accidents which had happened to *Lumpkin!* and been perpetrated by his driver could ever be traced back to Christopher Milton, that would be exactly the sort of scandal to bring the star down in the public estimation.

And yet Charles did not believe that Christopher Milton was directly involved. True, all the crimes turned out to the star's advantage, but Charles was convinced that the driver had either been acting off his own bat or on the orders of Dickie Peck. Either way, the motive had been a protective instinct, to keep the star from the harsh realities of life (like people disagreeing with him). Somehow Christopher Milton himself, in spite of all his verbal viciousness, retained a certain naïveté. He assumed that everything should go his way and was not surprised to find obstacles removed from his path, but his was more the confidence of a divine mission than the gangster's confidence in his ability to rub out anyone who threatened him. The star might have his suspicions as to how he was being protected, but he was too sensible to ask any questions about such matters. And far too sensible to take direct action. For a person so fiercely conscious of his public image it would be insane and, when it came to his career, Christopher Milton seemed to have his head very firmly screwed on.

The Friday performance was scrappy. The cuts had been only partly assimilated and the show was full of sudden pauses, glazed expressions and untidy musical passages where some of the band remembered the cut and some didn't. With that perversity which makes it impossible for actors ever to know what will or won't work onstage, the audience loved it. . . .

Charles was taking his make-up off at speed—even with the cuts, it was still a close call to the pub—when there was a discreet knock on his door. Assuming that someone must have got the wrong dressing-room, he opened it and was amazed to be confronted by his daughter Juliet and her husband Miles. What amazed him more was that Juliet, who had a trim figure and was not in the ordinary way prone to smocks, was obviously pregnant.

"Good heavens. Come in. . . . Sit down,' he added hastily, over-conscious of Juliet's condition. It confused him. He knew that everything about having children is a continual process of growing apart and could remember, when Frances first brought the tiny baby home, the shock of its separateness, but seeing his daughter pregnant seemed to double the already considerable gulf between them.

'Enjoyed the show very much,' Juliet volunteered.

'Oh good,' Charles replied, feeling that he should have kissed her on her arrival, but that he'd been too surprised and now he had missed the opportunity (and that the whole history of his relationship with his daughter had been missed opportunities to show affection and draw close to her). 'I didn't know you were coming. You should have let me know. I could have organised tickets,' he concluded feebly, as if free seats could compensate for a life-time of non-communication.

'I didn't know I was coming till today. Miles had to come to a dinner in Bristol and then I was talking to Mummy yesterday and she said you were in this show and I thought I'd come and see it.'

That gave him a frisson too. He had not told Frances about *Lumpkin!* How had she found out? At least that meant she was still interested in his activities. He couldn't work out whether the thought elated or depressed him.

'I didn't see the show, of course,' Miles stated in the plonking consciously-mature manner he had. 'I had to attend this dinner of my professional body.'

Charles nodded. He could never begin to relate to his son-in-law. Miles Taylerson did very well in insurance, which was a conversation-stopper for Charles before they started. Miles was only about twenty-five, but had obviously sprung middle-aged from his mother's womb (though, when Charles reflected on Miles' mother, it was unlikely that she had a womb—she must have devised some other more hygienic and socially acceptable method of producing children). Miles and Juliet lived in a neat circumscribed executive estate in Pangbourne and did everything right. They bought every possession (including the right opinions) that the young executive should have and their lives were organised with a degree of foresight that made the average Soviet Five-Year-Plan look impetuous.

When Miles spoke, Charles took him in properly for the first time. He was dressed exactly as a young executive should be for a dinner of his professional body. Dinner jacket, but not the old double-breasted or now-dated rolled-lapel style. It was cut like an ordinary suit, in very dark blue rather than black, with a discreet braiding of silk ribbon. Conventional enough not to offend any senior members of the professional body, but sufficiently modern to imply that here was a potential pace-setter for that professional body. The bow tie was velvet, large enough to maintain the image of restrained panache, but not so large as to invite disturbing comparisons with anything flamboyant or artistic. The shirt was discreetly frilled, like the paper decoration on a leg of lamb. In fact, as he thought of the image, Charles realised that that was exactly what Miles looked like—a well-dressed joint of meat.

Recalling a conversation that Miles and he had had two years previously on the subject of breeding intentions, he could not resist a dig. 'When's the baby due?' he asked ingenuously.

'Mid-April.' Juliet supplied the information.

'You've changed your plans, Miles. I thought you were going to wait a couple more years until you were more established financially.'

'Well, yes....' Miles launched into his prepared arguments. 'When we discussed it, I was thinking that we would need Juliet's income to keep going comfortably, but of course, I've had one or two rises since then and a recent promotion, so the mortgage isn't taking such a big bite as it was, and I think the general recession picture may be clearing a little with the Government's anti-inflation package really beginning to work and so we decided that we could advance our plans a little.'

He paused for breath and Juliet said, 'Actually it was a mistake.' Charles could have hugged her. He spoke quickly to stop himself laughing. 'I'm sorry I can't offer you anything to drink . . . I don't keep anything here.' With a last act entrance and an adjacent pub, there didn't seem any need.

'Don't worry, I'm not drinking much, because of the baby.'

'And I had up to my limit at the dinner. Don't want to get nabbed on the M4.' The image came of Miles sitting at the dinner of his professional body, measuring out his drinks drop by drop (and no doubt working out their alcoholic content with his pocket calculator).

'You say you heard from your mother yesterday,' said Charles, with what attempted (and failed) to be the insouciance of a practitioner of modern marriage, unmoved by considerations of fidelity and jealousy.

'Yes.'

'How was she?'

'Fine.'

'How's the new boy friend?' He brought in the question with the subtlety of a sledge-hammer.

'Oh, what do you . . .?' Juliet was flustered. 'Oh, Alec. Well, I don't know that you'd quite call him a boy friend. I mean, he just teaches at the same school as Mummy and, you know, they see each other. But Alec's very busy, doesn't have much time. He's a scout-master and tends to be off camping or climbing or doing arduous training most weekends.'

Good God. A scout-master. Frances must have changed if she'd found a scout-master to console her. Perhaps she'd deliberately looked for someone as different as possible from her husband.

Juliet tactfully redirected the conversation, a skill no doubt refined by many Pangbourne coffee mornings. 'It must be marvellous working in a show with Christopher Milton.'

'In what way marvellous?'

'Well, he must be such fun. I mean, he comes across as so . . . nice. Is he just the same off stage?'

'Not exactly.' Charles could also be tactful.

But apparently Christopher Milton united the Taylersons in admiration. Miles thought the television show was 'damn funny' and he was also glad 'that you're getting into this sort of theatre, Pop. I mean, it must be quite a fillip, career-wise.'

'What do you mean?'

'Well, being in proper commercial theatre, you know, West End, chance of a good long run, that sort of thing. I mean, it's almost like having a regular job.'

'Miles, I have done quite a few shows in the West End before, and if I have spent a lot of my life going round the reps, it's at least partly because I have found more variety of work there, more interest.'

'But the West End must be the top.'

'Not necessarily. If you want to be a star, I suppose it might be, but if you want to be an actor, it certainly isn't.'

'Oh, come on, surely everyone in acting wants to be a star.'

'No, actors are different. Some want to open supermarkets, some just want to act.'

'But they must want to be stars. I mean, it's the only way up. Just as everyone in a company wants to be managing director.'

'That principle is certainly not true in acting, and I doubt if it's true in the average company.'

'Of course it is. Oh, people cover up and pretend they haven't got ambitions just because they see them dashed or realise they haven't got a chance, but that's what everyone wants. And it must be the same in the theatre, except that the West End stars are the managing directors.'

'If that's the case, where do I come on the promotion scale?'

'I suppose you'd be at a sort of . . . lower clerical grade.' And then, realising that that might be construed as criticism, Miles added, 'I mean, doing the job frightfully well and all that, but sort of not recognised as executive material.'

They were fortunate in meeting the managing director on the stairs. Christopher Milton was leaving alone and, suddenly in one of his charming moods, he greeted Charles profusely. Miles and Juliet were introduced and the star made a great fuss of them, asking about the baby, even pretending to be interested when Miles talked about insurance. They left, delighted with him, and Charles reflected wryly that if he'd wanted to organise a treat, he couldn't have come up with anything better.

Christopher Milton's mood of affability remained after they'd gone. 'Fancy a drink?'

'Too late. The pubs have closed.'

'No, I meant back at the hotel.'

'Yes. Thank you very much.' Charles accepted slowly, but his mind was racing. The offer was so unexpected. If Christopher Milton were behind the accidents which had been happening over the past weeks and if he knew that Charles had been inspecting his car the night before, then it could be a trap. Or it could be an innocent whim. Acceptance was the only way of finding out which. And Charles certainly felt like a drink.

'Good. I've got a cab waiting at the stage door.'

'I thought you usually had your car.'

'Yes. Unfortunately my driver had an accident last night.'

The intonation did not sound pointed and Charles tried to speak equally casually. 'Anything serious?'

'Got a bang on the head. Don't know how it happened. He'll be in hospital under observation the next couple of days, but then he should be okay.'

'Do you drive yourself?'

'I do, but I don't like to have that to think about when I'm on my way to the theatre. I do quite a big mental build-up for the show.' Again the reply did not appear to have hidden layers of meaning. No suspicion that Charles was mildly investigating the accident to Pete Masters.

In his suite at the hotel Christopher Milton found out
Charles' predilections and rang for a bottle of Bell's. It
arrived on a tray with a bowl of cocktail biscuits. The star
himself drank Perrier water. '... but you just tuck into
that.'

Charles did as he was told and after a long welcome
swallow he offered the biscuits to his host.

'I don't know. Are they cheese?'

Charles tried one. 'Yes.'

'Then I won't, thanks.'

There was a long pause. Charles, who had the feeling
he was there for a purpose, did not like to initiate a topic
of conversation. Christopher Milton broke the silence.
'Well, how do you think it's going?'

'The show? Oh, not too bad. A lot of work still to be
done.' Clichés seemed safer than detailed opinions.

'Yes. This is the ugliest part.' Christopher Milton paced
the room to use up some of his nervous energy. 'This is
where the real work has to happen.' He stopped suddenly.
'What do you think of the cuts?'

'Cuts were needed.'

'That tells me nothing. We both know cuts were
needed. I'm asking what you thought of the cuts that were
made.'

'Well, it depends. If you're thinking of how much sense
we're now making of Goldsmith's play—'

'We're not. We're thinking of the audience. That's what
theatre's about—the people who watch the stuff, not the
people who write it.'

'I agree with you up to a point, but—'

'What you're trying to say is that the cuts could have
been spread more evenly, that I myself got off pretty
lightly. Is that it?'

'To an extent, yes.' Asked a direct question, Charles
felt bound to give his real opinion.

'I thought you'd think that. I bet they all think that,
that it's me just indulging my oversized ego.' Charles
didn't confirm or deny. 'Go on. That's what they think.
That's what you think, isn't it?'

The sudden realisation came that all the star wanted

that evening was someone to whom he could justify himself. The fact that it was Charles Paris was irrelevant. Christopher Milton was aware of the bad feeling in the cast and he wanted to explain his actions to someone, to make him feel better. Obviously he had more sensitivity to atmosphere than Charles had given him credit for. 'All right,' Charles owned up, 'I did think other cuts would have been fairer.'

Christopher Milton seemed relieved that he'd now got a point of view against which to deliver his prepared arguments. 'Yes, and I bet every member of the cast is sitting in his digs tonight saying what a bastard I am. Well, let me tell you, all I think is whether or not this show is going to be a success, and I'm going to do my damndest to see that it is. That's my responsibility.

'You see, *Lumpkin!* just wouldn't be on if I weren't in it. *She Stoops to Conquer*'s been around for years. No commercial management's likely to revive it unless they suddenly get an all-star cast lined up. I suppose the National or the RSC might do a definitive version for the A-level trade, but basically there's no particular reason to do it now. But I said I was interested in the project and the whole band-wagon started.

'Now we come to the point that I know you're thinking—that we're buggering up a fine old English play. No, don't deny it, you're a kind of intellectual, you're the sort who likes literature for its own sake. What I'm trying to tell you, to tell everyone, is to forget what the play was. We're doing a show for an audience in 1975. And that, in your terms, is probably a debased audience, an audience force-fed on television. Their ideal night out at the theatre would probably be to see 'live' some soap opera which they see twice a week in the privacy of their sitting-rooms. Okay, that's the situation. I'm not saying it's a good situation, it's just the way things are, and that's the audience I'm aiming for.

'Because of television, I'm one of the people they want to see. And they want to see a lot of me. They don't give a bugger about the twists and turns of Goldsmith's quaint old plot. They want to see Lionel Wilkins of *Straight Up,*

Guv, simply because he's something familiar. I've only realised this since we started playing the show in front of audiences. That's why I stopped playing Lumpkin rustic—oh, yes, I saw the expression of disapproval on your face when I did that. But I am right. Give the audience what they want.'

'All right, I agree they want to see you, but surely they'd be even more impressed if they saw your range of abilities, if they saw that you could play a very funny rustic as well as Lionel Wilkins.'

'No, there you're wrong. They want what they recognise. Popular entertainment has got to be familiar. This is a mistake that a lot of young comedians make. They think the audience wants to hear new jokes. Not true, the average audience wants to hear jokes it recognises. No, in this show they see sufficient variety in me, they see me sing and dance—most of them probably didn't know I could do that—but they never lose sight of Lionel Wilkins, and it's him they came for. And it's my business to give them Lionel Wilkins.

'So, when I said to Mark Spelthorne this morning that I felt responsbile for the entire company, I meant it. It's up to me to hold this company together and if that looks like just ego-tripping, well, I'm sorry.'

Charles couldn't think of anything to say. He had been surprised to hear such a cogently reasoned justification and, although he could not agree with all the arguments, he could respect it as a point of view. Christopher Milton himself obviously believed passionately in what he said. He broke from the unnatural stillness he had maintained throughout his exposition and started his restless pacing again. He stopped by a sofa and began rearranging the cushions. 'And it's the same reason, my duty to the audience, which makes me so concerned about my public image. I just can't afford to do anything that lowers me in their estimation.

'Oh, don't look so innocent, as if you don't know why I've moved on to this subject. People think I'm blind, but I see all the little looks, the raised eyebrows, the remarks about me putting on the charm. Listen, my talent, wherever it came from, is all I've got. It's a commodity and, like any other commodity, it has to be attractively packaged. I have to be what the public wants me to be.'

'Even if at times that means not being yourself?'

'Even if that means most of the time not being myself. That's the way of life I've chosen.'

'It must put you under incredible strain.'

'It does, but it's what I've elected to do and so I must do it.'

This messianic conviction seemed almost laughable when related to the triviality of *Lumpkin!*, but it was clear that this was what made Christopher Milton tick. And though the strength of his conviction might easily overrule conventional morality, he was never going to commit any crime whose discovery might alienate the precious audience whom he saw, almost obsessively, as the arbiters of his every action.

Charles left the Holiday Inn, slightly unsteady from the whisky, but with the beginnings of an understanding of Christopher Milton.

Twelve...

THE LIGHTS WERE still on in Julian's flat when Charles got back there, though it was two o'clock in the morning. Julian himself was in the front room, marooned wretchedly on an island of bottles, glasses and ash-trays. 'Oh, Charles, thank God you've come back. I need someone to talk to. It's started.'

'Started?'

'The baby.'

'Oh yes.' He nearly added 'I'd completely forgotten', but decided that might show an unwelcome sense of priorities.

'Waters broke, or whatever it is they do, about nine. I took her down to the hospital, they said nothing'd happen overnight, suggested I came back to get some sleep. Sleep, huh!'

'She'll be okay.'

'Yes, I'm sure she will, but that doesn't make the time till I know she is any easier. It's like quoting the statistics of normal childbirths, it doesn't make you any more convinced that yours is going to be one.'

'No. Well, you have a drink and keep your mind off it.'

'Drink, huh, I've had plenty of drinks.' Julian was playing the scene for all it was worth. Charles had the feeling that he often got with actor friends in real emotional situations, that they rose to the inherent drama and, though their feelings at such moments were absolutely genuine, their acting training was not wasted.

'Oh God,' Julian went on, 'the waiting. It's much worse than a first night.'

'For a small Paddon it is a first night.'

'Yes. Oh God!'

'Talk about something else. Take your mind off it.'

'All right. What shall we talk about?'

'The Irish situation? Whether *Beowulf* is the work of one or more writers? The Football League? Spinoza's *Ethics*? Is pay restraint compatible with democracy? Is democracy compatible with individual freedom? Is individual freedom compatible with fashion? Is fashion compatible with the Irish situation? Do stop me if you hear anything that sounds interesting.'

'Nothing yet. Keep talking.'

'You sod.'

'All right. Let you off. Tell me what you've been doing all day. I'm sure the wacky world of a pre-London tour must be more interesting than a day of rehearsal in a resident company.'

'Yes, I suppose today has been quite eventful. Desmond Porton of Amulet came down last night to pass sentence.'

'And are you still going in?'

'Oh yes, but today has been spent disembowelling the show.'

'Ah, that's familiar. A different show every night. Oh, the thrills of the open road.'

'You sound very bourgeois as you say that.'

'Well, I am. Respectable. Look at me—regular company, in the same job for at least six months. Married. . . .'

'Prospective father. . . .'

'Oh God!'

'I'm sorry. I'm meant to be taking your mind off that. I wonder what that makes you in the hierarchy.'

'What?'

'Being in a resident company. I suppose it's not quite a managing director but it's better than a lower clerical grade. A sort of rising young executive. Middle management, that's probably the level.'

'What are you talking about?'

'Nothing. I'm sorry. I'm a bit pissed.'

'Well, get stuck into that whisky bottle and get very pissed.'

'Okay.'

'Who have you been drinking with until this time of night?'

'With no less than Christopher Milton. The Star. Tonight I was given the honour of being the repository of his guilty secrets.'

'Not all of them, I bet.'

'Why, what do you—oh, of course, you knew him.' Spike's words of earlier in the day suddenly came back. 'You knew him before he was big.'

'Yes, I had the dubious pleasure of being with him in the first company he went to as an adult actor. He'd done quite a lot as a child, but this was his first job as a member of a company. Cheltenham, it was.'

'How long ago was this?'

'I don't know. Fifteen years—no, twenty. I remember, I celebrated my twenty-first birthday there.'

'Christopher Milton must have been pretty young.'

'Eighteen, I suppose.'

'No, fourteen. He's only thirty-four now.'

'My dear Charles, you must never allow yourself to be a victim of the publicity men.'

'What do you mean?'

'Christopher Milton is thirty-eight, at least.'

'But it says in the programme—'

'Charles, Charles, you've been in the business too long to be so naï. As you know, in this game everyone gets to play parts at the wrong age. People who play juveniles in the West End have almost always spent ten years grafting round the provinces and are about forty. But it doesn't have quite the right ring, does it? So when Christopher Milton suddenly became very big, he suddenly shed four years.'

'I see. It figures. Do you remember him from that time?'

'Difficult to forget.'

'What—the star bit?'

'Oh yes, give him his due, he never made any secret of what he wanted to be. He spent a good few years rehearsing for the big time.'

'Was he good?'

'Very good. But no better than any number of other young actors. Indeed there was another in the company at the time who was at least as good. He'd come from the same drama school, also done the child star bit—what was his name? Garry Warden, that was it. And who's heard of that name now? I don't know what happens to the products of the stage schools. They almost always vanish without trace....'

'Perhaps most of them haven't got Christopher Milton's single-mindedness.'

'Single-mindedness is a charitable word for it. God, he was terrible. Put everyone's backs up. Used to do charming things like ringing up other actors in the middle of the night to give them notes. And as you know it's very difficult to have that sort of person in a small company.'

'Did he drive everyone mad?'

'Funny you should say that.' Julian held his glass up to the light and looked through it pensively. 'No, he drove himself mad.'

'What do you mean?'

'He had a breakdown, complete crack-up. Couldn't live with an ego that size, maybe.'

'What form did the breakdown take?'

'Oh, the full bit. None of this quiet sobbing in corners or sudden keeling over in the pub. It was the shouting and screaming that everyone was trying to murder him sort. He barricaded himself in the dressing-room with a carving knife. I tell you, it was the most exciting thing to happen in Cheltenham since the Ladies' College Open Night.'

'Did he go for anyone with the knife?' Charles was beginning to feel a little uncomfortable.

'Went for everyone. One of the stage staff got a nasty gash on the forearm. It took three policemen to calm him down. Well no, not calm him down, hold him down. He was screaming blue murder, accusing us all of the most amazing things. Yes, it was a pretty ugly scene.'

'And did he come back to the company when he'd recovered?'

'No, he was taken off in a traditional little white van and that's the last time I saw him. Then suddenly four or five years ago I started reading all this publicity about the great new British star and there he was.'

'And you've no idea what happened to him after Cheltenham?'

'Not a clue. I suppose he went to some loony bin and got cured or whatever they do to people with homicidal tendencies.'

'Yes. Strange, I've never heard about that incident before.'

'Well, he's not going to go around advertising it. Lovable Lionel Wilkins, the well-known loony.'

'No, but it's the sort of story that gets around in the business.'

'Probably he's deliberately tried to keep it quiet. I suppose there aren't many people who would know about it. The Cheltenham company was pretty small—what was it the director used to call us? "A small integrated band." A cheap integrated band, anyway. God, when I think of the money they used to give us, it's a wonder we didn't all die of malnutrition.'

'You don't still see any of them?'

'No, not for years. I should think a lot of them have died from natural causes—and one or two drunk themselves to death.'

'Can you remember who was in that company?'

'Yes. Let me think—' At that moment the telephone rang. Julian leapt on it as if it were trying to escape. 'Hello. Yes, I am. What? When? But you said nothing would happen till the morning. Well, I know, but—what is it? Good Lord. Well, I . . . um . . . I mean. . . . Good Lord. But I wanted to be there. Can I come down? Look, it's only five minutes. No, I'll be there straight away. Good God, having effectively stopped me being there, you can bloody well keep them up for five minutes for me to see

them!' He slammed the receiver down and did a jaunty
little walk over to the fireplace. He turned dramatically to
Charles and threw away the line, 'A boy. Just a little boy.
Damian Walter Alexander Robertson Paddon.'

'Congratulations. That's marvellous.'

'Yes, it is rather good, isn't it? I must dash. The cow on
the phone wanted me to wait till the morning. God, I
should take her something.' He started frantically
scanning the room. 'I don't know what—grapes
or . . . where would I get grapes at three in the morning?
Oh, I'd better just—'

'Julian, I'm sorry, but who was in that company?'

'What?'

'In Cheltenham.'

'Oh look, Charles, I've got to rush. I—'

'Please.'

'Well, I can't remember all of them.' He spoke as he was
leaving the room. Charles followed him through the hall
and out of the front door to the car. 'There was Miriam
Packer, and Freddie Wort . . . and Terry Hatton
and . . . oh, what's the name of that terrible piss-artist?'

Charles knew the answer as he spoke. 'Everard
Austick?'

'Yes.'

'And was there a pianist called Frederick Wooland?'

'Good Lord, yes. I'd never have remembered his name.
How did you know? Look, I've got to dash.'

Julian's car roared off, leaving the road empty. And
Charles feeling emptier.

It was with a feeling of nausea, but not surprise, that he
heard next day that Mark Spelthorne had been found
hanged in his digs.

PART 4

Brighton

Thirteen...

IT SEEMED STRANGE to continue working with Christopher Milton after that. Or perhaps the strangeness lay in how easy it was, how much of the time it was possible to forget the grotesque suspicions which had now hardened in Charles' mind. And they were busy. *Lumpkin!* was scheduled to open at the King's Theatre on November 27th and the problems of re-rehearsing great chunks of the show were now exacerbated by extra rehearsals for Mark Spelthorne's understudy. (The management were dithering in London as to whether they should leave the part in the understudy's hands or bring someone else with a bit more name value. The boy who'd taken over wasn't bad... and he was cheaper than his predecessor... but was his name big enough...? Or with Christopher Milton above the title, did one perhaps not need any name value in the supports...? And after the cuts Young Marlow wasn't much of a part anyway.... The usual impersonal management decisions continued to be made a long way from the people they concerned.)

There was not much fuss over the death. Police were round asking about Mark's state of mind before the incident and there were rumours that some representatives of the company might have to attend the inquest, but the assumption of suicide was general. The coincidence of the failure of the radio pilot, the demise of the *Fighter Pilots* and troubles over *Lumpkin!* were thought to be sufficient motive. To a character like Mark Spelthorne,

155

whose life was driven by ambitions of stardom, this sequence of blows, with the implication that he was never going to make it in the way he visualised, could be enough to push him over the edge.

Even Charles found the explanation fairly convincing and tried to make himself find it very convincing. But other thoughts gate-crashed his mind.

An unwelcome logical sequence was forming there. What he had heard from Julian provided the thread which pulled all the wayward strands of the case together into a neat little bundle. Christopher Milton's history of mental illness was just the sort of thing that he would fight to keep from his adoring public. The mass audiences for popular entertainment are not the most liberal and broad-minded section of the population and they would not sympathise with anything 'odd'.

Everard Austick and the pianist Frederick Wooland had passed unnoticed through Dickie Peck's Approval of Cast net and Christopher Milton must have recoiled in shock when he saw them at rehearsals. They were links with the one episode in his past he was determined to keep quiet and so far as he was concerned, they had to be removed. Not killed or even badly injured but kept out of *Lumpkin!* Hence the airgun pellet and the shove which sent poor, pissed Everard downstairs. Charles kicked himself for being so blinkered about the evidence he had found in the Corniche. He had been looking for something to incriminate the driver and had found what he wanted, without considering that its location could be equally damning to the car's owner.

Because now he had no doubt of Christopher Milton's personal involvement. Apart from anything else, at the time of Mark's death, Dickie Peck was in London and the driver was in hospital. And everything became quite logical if the star was considered as potentially unbalanced. In his morbid self-obsession he saw everyone who challenged him as a serious threat to his personality and as such someone who should be removed or punished. It wasn't a case of Dickie Peck or the driver being over-protective; it was a paranoid man protecting himself. And it meant that Charles was dealing with a madman.

Only a madman would believe that he could continue to behave like that without ultimate discovery and disgrace. Only someone totally locked in his own world, someone who had lost touch with everyday reality. Christopher Milton's unshakable belief in his talent was matched by a belief in his immunity from discovery.

And he had been skilful. All of the crimes had the appearance of accidents or unrelated acts of violence. Charles felt certain that no one else in the company saw any pattern in them. And because *Lumpkin!* was on the move, it was unlikely that the different police forces involved would be aware of a sequence of crimes.

But now, with the death of Mark Spelthorne, the whole situation became more serious. Beating up people who get in your way is one thing; killing them puts you in a different league.

And Charles was still left with the dilemma of what he should do about it. Gerald's original instructions to him to protect the show and its star from sabotage now seemed grotesquely irrelevant. The situation had got beyond that. But he still did not have enough evidence to go to the police with a tale which must strain their credulity. The airgun pellets and the liquid paraffin were unsubstantiated evidence; he could have planted them, and anyway his own behaviour in snooping around the Holiday Inn car park could be liable to misinterpretation. He didn't have any proof that Christopher Milton was at the scene of most of the incidents.

He considered the possibility of talking directly to his suspect, but he couldn't imagine what he would say. A quiet word in the ear may stop a schoolboy from smoking behind the cycle sheds, but in a case of murder it's seriously inadequate. And if he was dealing with a potentially homicidal maniac, it was asking for trouble to draw attention to such suspicions. But the alternative was sitting and waiting for someone else to get hurt or even killed.

He wanted to discuss it with someone, but Gerald

Venables, who was the only suitable confidant, was too
involved in the situation and might panic.

So he would have to work it out on his own. He
thought through the known facts and wished there were
more of them. He made vague resolutions to find out as
much as he could about Christopher Milton's past and
current activities. One useful idea did come into his head.
He recollected that the first two crimes had been
committed between nine and ten in the morning and
suddenly tied this up with the unusual 'no calls before
ten-thirty' clause in the star's contract. It would be
interesting to find out what he did in the mornings. Was it
just that he liked a lie-in? That did not tally with the
voracious appetite for work he demonstrated the rest of
the day. He was prepared to stay up all night getting a new
number together and yet the day never began until half
past ten. That was worth investigating.

But it was one stray positive thought in a scrambled
mind. Everything else circled round uselessly, tangling
with emotions and producing nothing.

*   *   *

The Queen's Theatre, Brighton, was one of the great old
touring theatres of Britain. It had been built for more
spacious times, in the 1870s, before the cinema had
cheapened illusion by comparisons with the real thing.
When the Queen's was put up, people went to the theatre
for spectacle and they got it. Entertainments were built
round special effects—shipwrecks, fires and falling
buildings, magic, ghosts and live animals. And the
theatres were designed to cope.

The original stage machinery had been built for the
Rise and Sink method of set changing, whereby the stage
was made up of separate narrow sections, which could be
raised and lowered with different sets on them by an
elaborate system of pulleys and counterweights. There
was a cellar below the stage as deep as the proscenium was
high and above the audience's sight lines there was
equivalent space in the flying gallery. The complex of

girders and hawsers in the cellar was a feat of engineering comparable to one of the great Victorian railway bridges.

When the stage was designed, it had been equipped with the full complement of trap doors which were written into many plays of the period. Downstage were the corner traps, small openings used for the appearance or disappearance of one actor. Often these would be used as Star Traps, so called because the aperture was covered with a circle made up of triangular wooden segments like cake slices, hinged with leather on the outside, which would open like a star to deliver the actor on to the stage and then fall back into place.

Then there was the Grave Trap centre stage, which was always used for the Gravediggers' scene in *Hamlet*. And originally the theatre had had the most elaborate trap of all, the Corsican Trap, or Ghost Glide. This had been developed for the 1852 play *The Corsican Brothers* and enabled a ghost to rise from the grave as he moved across the stage.

Charles found it fascinating. He had always been intrigued by the mechanics of theatre and just being in the old building gave him that pleasantly painful feeling of hopeless nostalgia which always comes from the knowledge that, however much one exercises the imagination, however much one researches, it is never possible to know what earlier times were really like. He picked the brains of Len, the stage doorman, about the theatre's history and tried to spend as much time as he could alone there, sensing the building's past, hearing echoes of old triumphs, tantrums and love affairs.

But it was not easy to indulge this sentimentality. For one thing, the theatre had undergone many changes. The divided stage had been replaced in the forties and now most of the old equipment was boarded over. Only the Star Trap on the fore-stage was still kept working for the annual pantomime appearances of the Demon King (complete no doubt with miscued puff of smoke).

Then again the frantic re-rehearsal schedule for *Lumpkin!* was not conducive to luxuriating in nostalgia. But, most of all, the looming problem of what should be done about his knowledge of Christopher Milton's criminal activities kept Charles' mind naggingly full.

As in the other towns of the tour, the local Press greeted the arrival of *Lumpkin!* in Brighton with a big spread about the show's star. There was a photograph of Christopher Milton in one of his lovable poses and the column was headed 'BACK TO SCHOOLDAYS FOR LIONEL WILKINS.' Intrigued, Charles read on.

Lovers of television's *Straight Up, Guv* are in for a surprise this week at the Queen's Theatre when they see the show's lovable star Christopher Milton in a different rôle as an eighteenth-century rogue by the name of Tony Lumpkin.

'Actually, he's not that different from Lionel,' confides boyish 34-year-old Christopher. 'They're both conmen. I think, if anything, Tony Lumpkin is slightly more successful than Lionel. Well, let's face it—that wouldn't be difficult.'

Offstage, Christopher Milton is nothing like his bungling television counterpart. He is a hard-working performer with a great belief in the live theatre. 'Television is strange,' he muses. 'It's in one way the most intimate of the media, because everything you do on it is very small, you know, just for the camera, and because the viewers are just sitting in their livingrooms to watch. And yet in a strange way, for the performer, it's a distant feeling playing to a camera, even when there's a studio audience. It doesn't bear comparison with the contact you can get with a live theatre audience. That's electrifying, intoxicating, magic.'

For Christopher, being in Brighton is almost like coming home. 'I spent seven years of my life here at Ellen da Costa's Stage School. I came when I was a very young ten-year-old and left when I went into full-time professional theatre. In many ways, Ellen taught me all I know. I think she's retired now, but I certainly hope to see her while I'm in Brighton. I hope she'll come and see the show—and no doubt rap me over the knuckles for sloppy enunciation! She used to be very hot on enunciation. I can't think that she'd approve of Lionel Wilkins' style of speech....'

The article went on to complete the plug for *Lumpkin!* with information about Carl Anthony and Micky Gorton. It made no mention of Mark Spelthorne's death. But then the whole thing read like an Identikit PR interview which had been prepared long in advance.

Still, the information about the stage school was interesting. If the key to Christopher Milton's behaviour lay deep in his past, then it might be worth paying a visit to Miss Ellen da Costa.

The rehearsals were hard. They started with a ten-thirty call on the Monday morning and it was like working on a new show. Wally Wilson's typewriter had been busy and few scenes had escaped 'improvement'. The charming cadences of Goldsmith's lines had now completely vanished and were replaced by the staccato banality of television comedy. There was more work for everyone. At enormous cost, the band had special rehearsals with Leon Schultz. The choreographer kept snaffling dancers away to learn new routines in the theatre bar. Actors were rarely seen without scripts in their hands as they tried to flush the old lines out with the new. Wherever there was a piano it was surrounded by a knot of actors struggling to pick up altered songs. The atmosphere was one of intense pressure.

But surprisingly it was cheerful. The company seemed more united than ever. And this was almost solely due to Christopher Milton. His enthusiasm was infectious and he inspired everyone to greater and greater efforts. He made them think that they were working on the greatest show that had ever happened and that every change was only going to make it that much greater. Charles could not help admiring the Pied Piper strength of the man's personality. The company was carried along on the wave of his vitality. Even the previous doubters, like Winifred Tuke, made no more comments on the evisceration of

Oliver Goldsmith. The triumph of the Christopher Milton was total.

He was everywhere. David Meldrum no longer even made a pretence of directing. He acted as a glorified messenger boy for the star, organising rehearsal schedules as instructed and fixing the details of the increasingly elaborate technical side of the show.

Christopher Milton shared Charles' fascination for the mechanics of theatre and seemed to feel the magic of the old building. But he didn't just want to stand and dream while a sense of history seeped into him; he wanted to recapture that history and recreate the splendours of Victorian illusion. The Star Trap was quickly enlisted into the Chase sequence to fire Tony Lumpkin on to the stage from the bowels of the earth. (It was hoped to accompany this entrance with a flash from an electrically-fired maroon, but with the IRA bombers again in action, managements were nervous of sudden bangs in their theatres.) Moments later, Tony Lumpkin descended from the flies on a Kirby wire, then shot behind a tree only to reappear within seconds (thanks to the judicious use of a double) rising from the Grave Trap flanked by two eighteenth-century go-go dancers. The sequence was a far cry from *She Stoops to Conquer*, but it was moving towards the Chaplinesque quality the star wanted. Of course as the business got more and more detailed, so it expanded and yet more of the original plot had to be cut to accommodate it. At the current rate of progress, by the time the show got to London it would have no more substance than a half-hour episode of *Straight Up, Guv*. 'This week lovable conman Lionel Wilkins fools some supporting actors into believing that a private house is a pub—with hilarious consequences.'

But *Lumpkin!* was beginning to work. Taking Christopher Milton's advice and forgetting Goldsmith, Charles began to see what was emerging, and it was something with enormous potential. In his own strange way, Christopher Milton was a considerable artist. His instinct for the theatrical and particularly the comic was unerring. Charles began to see the situation as a Faustian one in which the star was achieving earthly success at the cost of his immortal soul. The dark side of madness and crime was a necessary complement to the genius of the public image.

After a very hard day's rehearsal on the Tuesday Charles was leaving the theatre to grab a quick bite before the evening performance when he met Suzanne Horst. 'Ah,' she said accusingly, 'there you are. Have you asked him yet?'

'What?' His mind was completely blank. He could only remember Suzanne drunk in his arms at the time of Pete Masters' accident.

'About the interview. You said you'd ask him.'

'Oh, did I?' He tried to sound ingenuous and squirm out of it.

'Yes, and you didn't do it in Bristol, which means I've lost some time. So look, I want to do the radio interview this week. It's for Radio Brighton and I've promised them I'll do it while he's down here.' The last sentence was not an appeal for help from a position of weakness; it was a reproof to Charles for failing to discharge a duty. Suzanne was a sharply efficient young lady once again; the warmth of their last encounter was only a product of the drink. Either she had forgotten it or was determined that it should be forgotten. 'So look, when am I going to be able to do it?'

'Well, I don't know,' he prevaricated. 'We're rehearsing very hard at the moment and—'

'Have you asked him yet?'

Faced with the point-blank question, Charles could only admit he hadn't.

Suzanne Horst gave a contemptuous grunt. 'Do you realise, you've wasted a lot of my time. I thought you were asking him.'

'I'm sorry,' he mumbled inadequately, trying to remember how he'd got into the position of agreeing to help her. 'Does that write off the magazine article as well?'

'No, it only slows that down too.' Her mind did not accommodate the idea of failure. 'But I've been doing quite a lot of background research on it.'

'Oh.'

'Yes, I went to see the old lady who ran his stage school, that sort of thing.' A firm reminder to Charles that that was his next priority. He started to make leaving noises, but did not escape without the final rap over the knuckles. 'I'm very disappointed in you, Charles. I was relying on you. Now I'll have to try my own more direct methods.'

*   *   *

Maybe it was the meeting with Suzanne that decided Charles to present himself at the Ellen da Costa Stage School in the guise of a journalist, or maybe it was just the obvious rôle to take when seeking information. Some inner warning mechanism told him not to go as Charles Paris.

There were some good old-clothes shops near the station in Brighton and he had kitted himself out well. The suit was cheaply cut, but looked newish, and the tie was a touch of psychedelic bravado, too young for its wearer and too old to be fashionable. His hair was greyed and Brylcreemed back like raked grass. A pair of pebble glasses changed the shape of his face and made seeing almost impossible. He stained two fingers of his right hand yellow and bought a packet of cigarettes. He didn't shave and rubbed a little Leichner No. 16 on to darken his jowl. Then an unfamiliar after-shave to cover the grease-paint smell.

He studied the effect in the mirror and thought he looked sufficiently anonymous. The face that looked back at him was like a child's Potato Man, random features stuck on to a vegetable. He adopted a slightly hunched stance, as if shrinking from the cold. It looked all right.

Now just a name and a voice. He fabricated Frederick Austick from the names of the first two victims of the accidents, then decided it was too obvious and amended it to Alfred Bostock. Despite temptations to go fancy or double-barrelled, he stuck at that. He tried a few words in his *Moby Dick* voice ('Allegorically inconsistent'—

Coventry Evening Telegraph), but was more satisfied with the one he'd used as Bernard in *Everything in the Garden* ('Authentic suburban twang'—*Surrey Comet*).

He didn't really know who he was disguising himself from—the rest of the *Lumpkin!* company were rehearsing on the Wednesday morning—but as usual he felt more able to cope with a difficult task in character.

The Ellen da Costa Stage School had closed some years before, but its principal still lived in the building (and still kept her hand in by giving elocution lessons to the young people of Brighton who had impediments or social aspirations). The school was a tall Victorian private house off one of the sea-front squares. Its owner's reduced circumstances were indicated by the cluster of tenants' doorbells attached with varying degrees of permanency to the old front door frame. Charles pressed the one whose plastic window showed a copperplate 'Ellen da Costa' cut from a visiting card.

She answered promptly, a long gaunt lady in black, whose flowing dress and shawl combined with a tangle of hanging beads to make her look like a bentwood hatstand. Her hair was swept back in flamenco dancer style, as if to justify her Spanish surname, but the white line at the roots gave the lie to its sleek blackness. The skin of her face was drawn tight over her cheekbones, as if, like the hair, its tension was maintained by the system of asymmetrical combs at the back of the head. She was made up with skill, but a skill which belonged to an earlier age and survives now only in opera.

But she had style and must once have been a beautiful woman. Though probably seventy, she behaved with the assurance of a woman who has no doubt of her sexual magnetism. There was no coquetry, but a grace and dignity, heightened by her theatrical manner.

'Good morning,' she enunciated with the attention to each vowel and consonant which she had instilled into generations of young hopefuls.

'Hello, I'm Alfred Bostock.' He slipped easily into his *Everything in the Garden* twang. 'I'm a journalist. I'm researching an article on Christopher Milton and I'm here

because I've heard that you had so much to do with
shaping his early career.'

She laughed a clear, tinkling laugh, only shown to be
staged by the over-dramatic intake of breath which
followed it. 'Ah, dear Christopher. Everyone wants to
know about him.'

'Other members of the Press, you mean?'

'Yes, dear boy. There was the cub from the local rag,
then a charming American girl, and now you.'

'Yes, I hope you don't mind going over the ground
again.'

'Mind? But, *mon cher*, I am always delighted to speak
about my little ones. And when it is *the* one, the one of all
others who had the *je ne sais quoi*, the unknowable
something that is stardom, why should I refuse? We who
serve genius must do our duty. Do come in.'

Charles, who was beginning to find her language a bit
excessive, followed her up a couple of staircases to a dark
sitting-room. It needn't have been as dark as it was, but
much of the window was obscured by an Art Deco glass
fire-screen with a colourful design of a butterfly. The
splashes of pale green, blue and red which the sun cast
over the floor and furniture gave an ecclesiastical flavour
to the room and this was intensified by the rows of
photographs in ornate metal frames on the walls. They
looked like images of saints and youthful miracle-
workers, with their slicked hair and unearthly smiles.
They were presumably the 'little ones', the pupils who had
taken their theatrical orders under Miss da Costa's
guidance and gone on to work in the field.

Two untimely candles added to the stuffy atmosphere
of Italian Catholicism which the room generated. Every
surface was crowded with souvenirs, more tiny framed
photographs, dolls, masks, gloves, programmes, massed
untidily like offerings before a shrine.

The votaress sank dramatically into a small velvet
chair and lay back so that the candle-light played gently
over her fine profile. It reminded Charles of *Spotlight*
photographs of ten years before, when every actor and
actress was captured in a fuzzy light which picked out

their bones in a murk of deepening shadows. (Nowadays actors tend to be photographed as if they've just come off a building site or are about to start life sentences for rape.) 'Well,' she said, 'you want to ask me about Christopher.'

She didn't ask for any credentials, which was a relief, because Charles hadn't thought through the details of what Alfred Bostock was meant to be researching.

'Yes, I'm after a bit of background, you know, what was he like as a child?' Charles mentally practised his Alfred Bostock voice by repeating 'Ford Cortina', 'double glazing' and 'ceiling tiles' to himself.

'Christopher came to me when he was ten.' Ellen da Costa settled down to her recitation from *Lives of the Saints*. 'Just a scrap of a boy, but with that same appealing charm and, of course, the talent. Even then, when he was unformed, the talent was there. Quite exceptional. His parents had died, in a car crash, I think, and it was an aunt who brought him to me. Very self-possessed he was.'

'When was this that he first came to you?'

Ellen da Costa gave him a look for talking in prayers, but she answered his question, revealing that she had not been in on the shedding of four years considered necessary to the star's career.

She then continued at some length describing the evolution of the embryo talent under the ideal laboratory conditions of her school. Charles was beginning to feel sated with superlatives when she offered to illustrate her lecture with a collection of Press cuttings pasted into large blue ledgers.

They weren't very revealing. One or two good notices for the young Christopher Milton, but nothing which suggested a performer set to take the world by storm. Charles mentioned this to Ellen da Costa in suitably reverential tones.

'Ah well, the Press has never been notorious for its recognition of true quality, particularly in the theatre. I once knew an actor, ...' the pause was deliberately left long to summon up images of years of wild passion. '... a very great actor, who was nearly crucified by the critics. It

was a martyrdom, a true martyrdom, very *triste*. Pardon
my speaking so of your chosen occupation—' for a
moment Charles couldn't think what she was talking
about—'but in my experience the Press has never, in this
country anyway, had the *delicatesse* to understand the
workings of genius.'

Charles did not attempt to defend his assumed calling,
but murmured something suitable. 'Also,' she continued,
her finely modulated voice drawing out the final 'o'
almost to breaking point, 'perhaps Christopher was not
fully realised at first. The potential was there, massive
potential. Of course, with my experience I could see that, I
was *sympathique* to it, but it was slow to blossom. At first
there were others who appeared more talented than he,
certainly who attracted more public notice, more Press
reaction, more work.'

'They worked while they were here?

She at once became guarded, as if this were a patch of
coals over which she had been hauled before. 'Most stage
schools also act as agencies for child performers and a lot
of our pupils do a great deal of work, subject of course to
the legal restrictions of only working forty days in the year
and with adequate breaks. All the children are chap-
eroned and—'

But Charles was not writing a muck-raking article on
the exploitation of child actors, so he tactfully cut her
short, and asked if she would show him some of the early
photographs of Christopher Milton.

She obliged readily. 'Here are some from 1952.' They
looked very dated. Styles of period stage costume change
quite as much as current fashion and the starched ruffs
and heavy Elizabethan garments the children wore had
the same distant unreal quality as Victorian pornography.
'This is from a production of *Much Ado* my students did.
Christopher was playing Claudio.'

Charles took the photograph she proffered. Christopher Milton's face was instantly recognisable, even
under a jewelled and feathered hat. All twenty-three years
had done was to cut the creases deeper into his skin.

But it was the other two children who intrigued

Charles. They were beautiful. Their grace in the heavy costumes made them look like figures from an Elizabethan painting and showed up Christopher Milton as very twentieth century, almost gauche in doublet and hose. The girl had a perfect heart-shaped face and long-lashed eyes whose grave stare, even from the old photograph, was strongly sensual. She appeared to be looking at the boy, who returned her gaze with the same kind of intensity. He had the epicene grace which some adolescent boys capture before they coarsen into adults. The face was almost baby-like in its frame of long blond curls. The eyes were deep-set and powerful.

'Claudio,' Charles repeated after a long pause. 'That's not the best part in the play. Presumably this young man played Benedict?'

'Yes.'

'Was he good?'

'Yes, he was very good. He did a lot of film work in his teens. Gareth Warden, do you remember the name?'

'It rings a bell.' Yes, Julian Paddon had mentioned it and, now he saw the photograph, Charles realised that Gareth Warden had been in the film he'd caught the tail-end of on Jim Waldeman's television. That seemed so long ago it was like a memory from a previous incarnation. 'And the girl?'

'Prudence Carr. She was a clever little actress, so clever.'

'And she played Beatrice?'

'Yes.'

'Any idea what happened to her? Or to Gareth Warden, come to that?'

'I don't know, Mr Bostock. The theatre brings its share of heartbreaks to everyone who is involved in it.' She gave a long sigh, which was a good demonstration of the breath control so vital for elocution and which was also meant to imply a lifetime of theatrical heartbreaks. 'Neither of them did much so far as I know. Dear Garry had the misfortune of early success. It's so difficult for them to make the transition from playing child parts to adult ones. As you see, he was a beautiful boy. Perhaps he decided the theatre was not the career he wanted. *Je ne sais pas.* He hasn't kept in touch at all.'

'And the girl?'

'The same story. I haven't seen her since she left my care. Maybe she didn't go into the theatre.'

'She should have done. With looks like that. And if she could act as well as you say.'

'Ah, she was magic. But things change. Fate takes a hand. Maybe she settled down and got married. How many promising careers have been cut short by matrimony. And how many only started by the failure of matrimony,' she added mysteriously with a suffering gaze out of the window to some distant memory. 'But *c'est la vie.* Some rise and some fall. Of those three, all the same age, all so talented, one was chosen, one who was more talented, one who had the real magic of stardom, and that was dear Christopher. He triumphed and left his rivals standing.'

With recent knowledge of Christopher Milton's methods of leaving his rivals standing, Charles wondered if there was some story from the past which might show a parallel. 'Presumably, Miss da Costa, with three students who were so talented in the same area, there must have been moments of jealousy between them?' he probed.

'Ah, the young are always jealous. They are so afraid, they feel that if they are not the absolute best in the world, then they are the absolute worst. Only with time can they understand that most are destined to be fairly good or fairly bad, that the world is made up of mediocrity and that only a chosen few, like dear Christopher, will be the best.'

Charles tried to move her from generalisations to the specific. 'You mean they were jealous of each other?'

'But of course. They would not be normal if they weren't.'

'And was that jealousy ever expressed in violence?'

'Violence?' Her eyes widened and again she stiffened as if he were trying to find scandal. 'Of course not. I kept a respectable school, Mr Bostock. Nowadays, if one can believe the newspapers, violence in the classroom is commonplace. I did not allow it in my school.'

'No, of course not. That's not what I meant.' Charles covered his retreat clumsily, realising that he wasn't going to get any answers to that question. But then it struck him that a bit of well-placed journalistic boorishness might be productive. 'Of course, Miss da Costa, another thing we keep reading about in the newspapers is sex in the classroom.'

'Sex.' She gave the word Lady Bracknell delivery.

'Yes, I mean, a group of young adolescents together, it's inevitable that they're going to form relationships. I was wondering, I mean, say these three youngsters, was there also some kind of emotional attachment between them?' He was glad he had come in disguise. Charles Paris could never have managed this crudeness of approach.

The question touched a nerve which had apparently been exposed before. 'Mr Bostock, I don't think there is any need to go over this ground again. The investigation by the local education authority in 1963 revealed that I was quite blameless in that matter.'

Intriguing though it was, Miss da Costa's dark secret had no relevance to his current enquiries, so Charles tried to retrieve some of the ground he had lost. 'I'm sorry, I think you misunderstand me. I'm not talking about 1963. As you know, I'm interested only in Christopher Milton. What I meant by my question was, was there maybe some early schoolboy romance we could mention? You know, the women readers go for all that stuff. "My first romance." It was a perfectly innocent enquiry.'

It worked. 'Oh, I see.' She sat back. 'I'm sorry, but I have had cause in my life to be somewhat wary of the Press. When one has figured in the private life of the great ...' Again she left the hint of her wildly romantic past dangling to be snapped up by anyone interested. Charles wasn't, so she continued after a pause. 'Well, of course, when you are speaking of young people, of beautiful young people, yes, *l'amour* cannot be far away. Oh, I'm sure at one time or another, all three of them were in love with each other. All such sensitive creatures. Yes, I have seen the two boys wildly, madly in love. I have seen them both look at Prudence in a way ... in a way one can recognise if one has seen it directed at oneself. Then one understands. Ah, I sometimes wonder if one has loved at all if one has not heard a lover's voice reciting Swinburne soft in one's ear. Don't you?'

He thought that Charles Paris' and Alfred Bostock's answers to that question might well be identical, so he tried to get the conversation back on the subject and avoid the Ellen da Costa Anthology of Love Poetry. 'Hmmm,' he offered, in a way that he hoped dismissed Swinburne. 'I was wondering, do you know if either of the affairs with Prudence continued after they left the school?'

'Mr Bostock, I do not like your word "affair"; it implies impropriety at my school.'

'I'm sorry. You're misunderstanding me again. I just meant, you know, the ... friendships.'

'That, Mr Bostock, I'm afraid I don't know. For the first year after they left, I heard a little of them—well, that was inevitable. I act as agent for all my pupils for their first year out of school.'

'You mean you put them under exclusive contract?'

'I prefer to think that I protect them from some of the sharks and exploiters in the agency business. But after the year, I heard nothing of Garry or Prudence. Of course, I heard a great deal about Christopher. Everywhere these days, one hears about Christopher. Did you see this in the local paper?' She opened one of the blue ledgers and pointed to the cutting from the previous day's paper. It was already neatly glued in. Charles found the promptness of its filing sad. It opened a little window on to the great emptiness of the old lady's life. He told her that he had seen the article and rose to leave.

Now she seemed anxious to detain him. 'Did you notice, he said in the interview that he'd try to come and see me while the show's down here.'

'Yes. Well, I believe that the company are doing a great deal of rehearsal at the moment.'

'Oh yes, I fully understand.' She reclined elegantly in her chair, the High Priestess of the Cult, prepared to wait forever for her Mystic Experience.

Fourteen...

CHARLES RANG JULIAN Paddon from a phone-booth on the front. 'Hello, how's the family?'

'Sensationally well. Damian has inherited my own innate sense of the theatre. I went to see them yesterday and he shat all over the nurse who was changing him. What timing. I think he'll grow up to be a critic.'

'And Helen?'

'Fine. Uncomfortable, which is I believe a feature of the condition, but extremely cheerful. Normal cervix, I understand, will be resumed as soon as possible. No hint of purple depression or whatever it is. Can't wait to get home.'

'When will that be?'

'Monday, I hope.'

'Listen, Julian, I wanted to pick your brains again. You remember we were talking last week about the old Cheltenham company you were in with Christopher Milton.'

'Oh yes.'

'You did say that an actor called Gareth Warden was also in the company?'

'Yes.'

'Seen anything of him since?'

'No. Why do you ask?'

'Oh, it's just something I'm trying to work out. You've no idea what happened to him?'

'Vanished off the face of the earth so far as I know.'

Julian's words gave substance to a thought which had been forming in Charles' mind. Christopher Milton tended to make people who challenged him 'vanish off the face of the earth'. Was the key to the current set of crimes in a crime which had been committed long before?

'Hmmm. I see. Another thing—you don't remember by any chance what Christopher Milton's sex-life was like at the time?'

'Good God. What do you want—times, dates, with whom, number of orgasms achieved? It was twenty years ago, Charles. It's hard enough to remember what my own sex life was like.'

'I mean just in general terms.'

'Blimey. Well, let me think—I don't remember him being gay, though I could be wrong. I don't remember him taking up with anyone in the company—mind you, there wasn't much spare there, they tended to get snapped up pretty quickly. I don't even recall a sort of regular popsie coming down for weekends. Oh, it's a long time ago. I honestly don't know, Charles. I mean, keeping a track of actors' love-lives is like doing a National Census of rabbits. Sorry, I just can't remember.'

'Oh well, never mind. And you can't ever recall hearing him speak of a girl called Prudence Carr?'

'Nope.'

'Does the name mean anything to you?'

'Nope.'

'Oh. Well, I—ooh, one last thing—when he had his breakdown, was it caused by anything personal, you know, a girl who'd chucked him or. . . .'

'I don't think so, Charles. I think it was solely due to the fact that the world did not at that time share his inflated opinion of himself. As I remember him, sex was a long way down his list of priorities. In fact everything was a long way down his list of priorities—except for his career and becoming a star.'

The strain of the extra rehearsals and the difficulties of remembering a continuously changing text began to show on the Wednesday evening performance. Perhaps the matinée was the last straw which made the cast suddenly realise how tired they were. Whatever the reason, the mood of united endeavour was replaced in a moment by an atmosphere of bad temper and imminent disintegration.

It was small things that went wrong. Lines were missed and lighting cues were slow. As the show progressed, the contagion spread and by the end everyone felt they were doing everything wrong. There weren't any major errors of the sort that an audience is likely to notice, but they worried the cast and undermined the communal confidence.

The Chase Scene was all over the place. Entrances were missed and special effects failed to function. The Star Trap didn't work. Because of other stage management crises, the crew forgot about it completely and Christopher Milton rushed down to the cellar to find the locking bar which held the wooden platform firmly in position and no sign of the four members of the crew who were meant to man the ropes and eject him on to the stage. As a result he had to rush back up on stage mouthing obscenities at everyone and make a very tame entrance from the wings. The comic timing of the scene's slapstick was ruined.

Even Charles didn't escape the epidemic of cack-handedness. He actually fell over in his first scene. To give him his due, it wasn't his fault. Because of the general panic of the stage management, including some local help who'd only been brought in that day, the rostrum on to which he had to move at a given point had not been anchored to the ground and was free-moving on its wheels. So, as soon as he put his foot on it, it sped away, forcing an ungainly splits movement which deposited him flat on his face. It got a good laugh from the audience, but, since it took place in the course of Tony Lumpkin's romantic song to Bet Bouncer, it was perhaps not the sort of laugh the show wanted.

The only person who came through the performance unscathed was Lizzie Dark. In fact, she was at her very best. She had an advantage. She was only eighteen

months out of Sussex University and still had a lot of
friends there who had come *en masse* to see her. They
were wildly partisan and applauded her every action. The
general mediocrity of the performance made her seem
even better and the reaction grew increasingly fulsome. It
was only a small group in the audience, but they were
noisy. At the curtain call, they screamed and shouted
'Bravos!' and 'Encores!' at her. It was an elaborate private
joke, recapturing no doubt the heady atmosphere of a
campus first night, and it was out of place in a
professional theatre. But Lizzie seemed to be carried
along by it, to be instantly transported back to amateur
night. She played to her gallery shamelessly.

Christopher Milton exploded as soon as the curtain
was down. Surprisingly he didn't turn on Lizzie or any
other of the cast who had miscued him or let him down.
He let the stage management have it. Of all the errors of
the show, it was his ignominious return to the stage from
the Star Trap which really rankled. He bawled them all
out. Four-letter words flew around as he lambasted their
incompetence, called them amateurs, provided a few
choice images of things he wouldn't trust them with and
some equally vivid ones of fates that would be too good
for them. This display of temper was the most violent
Charles had witnessed from the star and it made him
uncomfortable. The great hiss of anger came like steam
from a pressure cooker and before long the pressure
cooker was going to explode and scald everyone in sight.
Charles couldn't keep his knowledge to himself and do
nothing much longer.

The inefficiency which had characterised the performance continued. While the star was unleashing his
diatribe onstage, a group of schoolkids had somehow
eluded Len the stage doorman's vigilance and invaded the
dressing-rooms. They had only been driven by enthusiasm and were in fact fans of Christopher Milton, but he
was in no mood for one of his sudden switches to charm.
He added a few lacerating sentences against Len and said
he'd remain on stage until the fans had been cleared. The
rest of the cast shuffled sheepishly off to get changed.

Charles started to follow them. He was in a bad mood; the limping performance and the ensuing row had ruled out any possibility of getting to the pub before closing time. But just as he was at the pass door he noticed Christopher Milton going off into the wings and down the stairs to the cellar. Presumably just to have another look at the offending Star Trap. What made it interesting was that Lizzie Dark followed him.

There was another way down to the cellar backstage. Charles moved silently, though there was no one about. The cellar was lit by a couple of isolated working lights, but the vertical and horizontal girders of the old stage machinery made forests of shadow through which he could creep to a good spying position. Somewhere over the other side Spike or one of the stage crew was hammering nails into a broken flat, but he paid no attention to the intruders.

As Charles anticipated, Christopher Milton was looking balefully at the Star Trap mechanism. Four wooden beams boxed in the small platform on which the person to be ejected stood. The platform was in the up position, almost flush with the stage underneath the hinged Star top. The locking bar, a solid piece of two by four, was firmly in position, blocking any movement. The star slapped it petulantly. He seemed aware of Lizzie Dark's presence, but, though he spoke out loud, he did not speak to her. 'Sodding thing. Why we're stuck with this sort of old-fashioned crap I don't know. Four people to operate it. You'd think with a system of counter-weights, you could make it self-operating. Get this bloody locking bar out and leave it preset, so that it's ready when I am and not when the bloody stage crew are.'

'But,' Lizzie hazarded tentatively, 'if you took out the locking bar and had it down for too long someone onstage might step on and fall through.'

'Yes, so we're back relying on incompetents.' His anger had drained away, leaving him tired and listless.

'Christopher. . . .'

'Yes.'

'I wanted to apologise for tonight.'

'Eh?'

'That load of lunatics in the audience. My so-called friends. I'm afraid they did rather misbehave. It can't have made it any easier for you to concentrate.'

'Oh, never mind. There are good nights and bad nights.' His voice was philosophical and very tired. The violent outburst Charles had expected didn't come. That was what made being with Christopher Milton so exhausting. There was never any indication of which way he was going to jump.

'Well, I'm sorry. I shouldn't have played up to them. It was a bit unprofessional.'

'Never mind.' He put his arm round the girl's waist affectionately. 'We all have to learn.'

This avuncular, kindly Christopher Milton was a new one on Charles and he found it unaccountably sinister. The arm stayed round her waist as Lizzie asked, 'How do you think it's going, Christopher?'

'It's going all right. It'll be very good—if we all survive to see the first night.'

'Am I doing all right?'

'Yes, you're good. Could be better in bits.'

No actress could have resisted asking which bits.

'That song in the second half, the romantic one. There's a lot more to be got out of that.'

'Yes, I'm sure there is, but the trouble is, David never actually gives any direction and I'm not experienced enough to know what to do myself. . . . It's difficult.'

'I'll take you through it when I've got a moment.'

'Would you?'

'Sure. When? What's the rehearsal schedule tomorrow?'

'The afternoon's free. We're all meant to be in need of a rest.'

'And how.' The deep weariness in the two words reminded Charles of the intense physical pressure that the star had been under for the past months. 'But okay. Let's go through it tomorrow afternoon.'

'No, I don't want to take up your time. I—'

'Here. At three o'clock.'

'Well, if you really. . . .'

'I really.'

'Thank you. I'm sorry, I just feel so amateur in this company. I mean, it's jolly nice getting good jobs, but I've only done a year round the reps and I've got so much ground to make up.'

'Don't worry. You'll make it. You've got talent.'

'Do you really mean it?'

'I do. You'll be a big star. Probably bigger than me.'

'Come off it.'

'I'm serious. It's a long time since I've seen an actress who had your kind of potential. There was a girl I was with at drama school, but no one since then.'

'What was her name?'

'Prudence.'

'And what happened to her?'

'Ah.' There was a long pause, during which Charles felt that water, defying the laws of gravity, was being poured up his back. 'What does happen to talented girls who work with me?'

Christopher Milton moved suddenly. The hand on Lizzie Dark's waist was brought up sharply to her neck where his other hand joined it. Charles started forward from his hide to save her.

They didn't see him, which was just as well. Because far from being strangled, as he feared, Lizzie Dark was being passionately kissed. Charles melted back into the shadows. The hammering in the distance continued, but otherwise the cellar was silent as he crept out, feeling like a schoolboy surprised with a dirty book.

The next morning Alfred Bostock took over the case again. For the next part of the investigation it would not do to be recognised and, after the previous night's unsatisfactory spying, Charles wanted the comfort of disguise.

He'd hung around the stage door until Christopher Milton and Lizzie Dark left the building. They had come out separately and set off in opposite directions. Charles trailed Christopher Milton to the Villiers, his sea-front hotel. (It was so near the theatre that there was no point in having a car, even for a star.) That made him think that Lizzie at least was safe for the night. What had gone on in the cellar after he'd left fed his imagination. It was a good half-hour before they emerged, so most things were possible.

But the urgency of the case was inescapable. The star's violent outburst, the strangeness of his behaviour with Lizzie, and a vague but unpleasant idea of what had happened to Gareth Warden and Prudence Carr made Charles realise that he could dither no longer. And the most obvious thing to do was to find out what Christopher Milton did during that missing hour in the morning.

Charles was very organised. He got up at five o'clock after a disbelieving look at the alarm clock and started making up as Alfred Bostock.

At six-thirty he rang the Villiers. A night porter answered. Charles said he was ringing on behalf of Dickie Peck, Mr Milton's agent, and was Mr Milton up, he knew he sometimes got up very early. No, Mr Milton was not up. Yes, he was in the hotel, but he was sleeping. Yes, he was certain that Mr Milton had not gone out, because he'd been on all night. Yes, he thought it would be advisable if the representative of Mr Peck rang back later. Mr Milton normally ordered breakfast in his suite at eight o'clock. And, incidentally, the Villiers Hotel looked forward to Mr Peck's arrival later in the day.

At eight o'clock the representative of Mr Peck—who incidentally used the accent Charles Paris had used as Voltore in *Volpone* ('Lamentably under-rehearsed'— *Plays and Players*)—rang again and asked to be put through to Mr Milton. He was connected, but as soon as Christopher Milton spoke, there occurred one of those unfortunate cut-offs which are a feature of the British telecommunications system. Charles Paris, in a phone-booth on the sea-front opposite the Villiers Hotel, knew that his quarry was inside and was determined to follow him wherever he went. He had checked the entrances and exits and, unless Christopher Milton left through the kitchens (which would be more conspicuous than the main door in terms of witnesses), he would have to come out on to the front. Now it was just a question of waiting.

Charles sat in a shelter with a miserable-looking couple of old men who were realising their life-time's ambition of retiring to the south coast. They depressed him. It was cold. He saw himself with the deadly X-ray eye of a third person. A middle-aged actor play-acting on the front at Brighton. Someone who'd never managed to create a real relationship with anyone, a man whose wife was forced to take solace with a scout-master, a man whose daughter spoke the language of another planet, a man who would sink into death without even disturbing the surface of life, unnoticed, unmourned. How would he be remembered? As an actor, not for long. Maybe the occasional unfortunate accident might stick in people's minds: 'There was an actor I knew—what was his name?— Charles Paris, that's right, and he. . . .' Or would he just live on as a sort of Everard Austick, an archetypal heavy drinker in the mythology of the theatre? 'There was an incredible piss-artist in a company I was once in, bloke called Charles Paris, and he used to drink. . . .' No, he wasn't even an exceptional drinker, not the sort of wild alcoholic around whom Rabelaisian stories gathered. He drank too much, but not interestingly too much.

Perhaps it was the sea-front in winter that made him so introspective, but he found big questions looming in his mind, big unanswerable cliché questions, all the *whys?* and *why bothers?* and *what does it matters?* Life was very empty.

There was a man walking along the street towards the Villiers Hotel. Charles stiffened. Here at last was something, something real and tangible.

The man he saw was bald, with big ears. When he had seen them in Leeds, Charles had thought the ears looked like handles of a loving cup. The man had hardly registered in Bristol, Charles had just thought he looked like the one in Leeds, but now seeing him for the third time there was no question. It was the same man.

And each time the man had appeared near Christopher

Milton's hotel early in the morning. Charles felt he was near to solving the mystery of who did the star's dirty work.

He crossed the road and followed the bald man into the Villiers Hotel. He hadn't really planned his next move, but it was made easy for him. There was temporarily no one in Reception. The bald man rang for a lift. Charles stood by his side, assessing him. A bit old for a heavy, but he was well-built and had the bear-like shape of a wrestler. His mouth was a tight line and the eyes looked mean.

The lift came. The bald man got in and asked for the fourth floor. Charles, who hadn't acted in fifties detective films for nothing, also got in and asked for the fifth. There wasn't one. 'Oh, so sorry,' he said, feeling that this wasn't a very auspicious start. 'I mean the fourth—third.'

The bald man did not seem to notice his companion's gaucheness and Charles was decanted on the third floor. It was a matter of moments to find the stairs and scurry up to the fourth. He hid behind the fire-door and watched the bald man walk along the corridor to room 41, knock and enter.

Charles followed, treading noiselessly in the soft pile of the expensive carpet. He stopped by room 41 and put his ear to the door. He could hear two voices, one of them recognisably Christopher Milton's, but they were too far away for him to distinguish the words.

Anyway, he was in a rather exposed position for listening. A Hoover stood unattended in the corridor and muffled singing also indicated the presence of cleaners. He'd have to move quickly.

The cleaners had left a key with its heavy metal label in the door of room 42. He opened the door and sidled in.

He had expected an immediate confrontation with a suspicious cleaner but miraculously the suite was empty. He moved to the wall which was shared with room 41 and put his ear to it. They were still talking, but, though the speech was clearer, it was again impossible to hear individual words. The effect was of badly tuned radio.

Remembering another movie, Charles fetched a tooth-glass from the bathroom. Pressed against the wall it improved the sound quality, but still not enough to make it intelligible. People who paid for their privacy at the Villiers Hotel did not waste their money.

He was almost despairing when he thought of the balcony. A sea view was another of the perks for those who were prepared to pay the astronomical rates charged for a fourth-floor suite at the Villiers.

He slid the galvanised steel door back. The cold slap of air made him realise how grotesquely over-heated the hotel was.

The balcony of room 42 adjoined that of 41. Only a bar separated them. By sliding along the wall of the building, Charles could get very close to Christopher Milton's window and still remain out of sight from the room. The window was slightly open in reaction to the central heating. Charles could hear what was being said inside quite clearly.

He stood high above the sea-shore on a cold November morning in Brighton and listened.

Christopher Milton's voice came first, strangled with passion. '. . . And I can't stand the way they are always looking at me, always assessing me. I hate them all.'

'What do you mean, you hate them?' The other voice was toneless, without any emotion.

'I mean I want something to happen to them.'

'What?'

'I want them out of my way. The others went out of my way.'

'Yes.' The dry voice gave nothing. 'What do you want to happen to them?'

'I want them to die. I want them all to die.' He could hardly get the words out.

'Who are you talking about?'

'All of them.'

'Not all. We can't just kill them all, can we? Who do you really want dead?'

'Charles Paris.' The name was hissed out. 'I want Charles Paris dead.'

Fifteen...

AT THAT MOMENT someone came into the room behind Charles and let out an incomprehensible shriek. It was one of the cleaners, a slender Filipino girl in a blue nylon overall. She looked at him with widening black eyes. He had to think quickly. 'Room 32?' he offered. And then, to cover himself in case she knew the occupant of Room 32, 'Toilet? Toilet?' Unaccountably the words came out in a comedy sketch Spanish accent.

'Toilet,' the girl echoed, as if it were a word she had heard before, but did not understand.

'Si, si,' Charles continued insanely, 'dondo este el toilet?'

'Toilet,' the girl repeated, now uncertain whether she had actually heard the word before.

'Si, toiletto.' He thought adding the final 'o' might help, but it didn't appear to. The girl looked blank. Charles pointed to his fly as a visual aid to the word 'toilet'.

This time the girl understood. Or rather she misunderstood. Throwing her hands in the air, she cried 'Rape!' and rushed out into the corridor.

Charles followed at equal speed. He too wanted to get away in a hurry. Unfortunately the Filipino girl took his movement for pursuit and redoubled her screams. They rushed along the corridor in convoy, because she had chosen to run in the direction of the lifts. Doors opened behind them and bewildered faces stared. Charles decided he couldn't wait for the lift and took to the stairs. He managed to get out of the building without being stopped.

He sat in the shelter opposite the Villiers Hotel and tried to control the breath which was rasping in his throat. It wasn't only the physical effects of the chase that made him feel so shaky. It was also the unpleasant feeling which comes to people who have just heard a contract being taken out on their lives. He gasped and trembled and, although a diluted sun was now washing the sea-front, the morning seemed colder.

The two old men were still sitting in the shelter, overtly ignoring him, but with sly side-glances. They didn't depress him now. They were part of a humanity he did not want to leave. Dr Johnson's adage about the proximity of death concentrating the mind wonderfully was proving true. The depression he had felt so recently seemed a wicked affront to life, to all the things he still wanted to do. And yet within fifty yards of him a lunatic was giving a paid killer instructions to murder him.

It was ridiculous. He had that feeling he could recall from prep school of getting into a fight and suddenly realising that it was becoming more vicious than he'd expected and suddenly wanting to be out of it. Like a recurrent nightmare in which, after a long chase, he always capitulated and apologised and pretended it had all been a joke. But this was not a joke.

The question of what to do about the whole case had now taken on more than a dilettante interest. It had become an issue of red-hot urgency. But the answer didn't come any more readily.

Though the sequence of Christopher Milton's (or his hit-man's) crimes and their motives were now clear as daylight, Charles still had no real evidence. Just the gin bottle, the airgun pellets and the liquid paraffin, but none of those could be pinned on the criminals and none related to the most serious crimes.

He still needed positive proof of wrong-doing, Or, since he was apparently the next person to be done wrong to, positive proof of the intention to do wrong might be preferable. He decided to follow the bald man in the hope of catching him red-handed. (The details of how he would himself catch red-handed someone whose criminal

mission was to eliminate him he left for the time being.
They would supply themselves when the occasion arose.)

He counted his advantages and there weren't many.
First, he knew they were after him, so he was on his guard.
Secondly, he was in disguise and so could spy on them
without automatic discovery. Not much, but better than
nothing.

At about five past ten the bald man came out of the
hotel. He walked without suspicion, no furtive glances to
left and right. Charles had the advantage of hunting the
hunter.

The bald man was an ideal candidate for tailing. He
walked straight ahead at a brisk pace, not stopping to
look in shop windows or dawdling aimlessly. All Charles
had to do was to adjust his own pace to match and follow
along about fifty yards behind. Brighton was full of
shoppers and the pursuit was not conspicuous.

It soon became clear that the man was going to the
railway station. He walked briskly and easily up the hill,
fitter than his appearance suggested. Charles thought
uncomfortably of the strength he had seen in middle-aged
wrestlers on the television. It if came to direct physical
confrontation, he didn't reckon much for his chances.

The man didn't stop to buy a ticket. He must have a
return, because he showed something at the barrier. He
went on to Platform 4, for trains to London. At first
Charles was going to buy a single, but that showed a
depressing lack of faith in the outcome of his mission, so
he got a return.

He also bought a *Times* for burying his face in. Tabloid
newspapers, he decided, must be unpopular with the
criminal fraternity; they hide less.

The train came soon, which implied that the bald man
knew the times and was hurrying for this specific one.
Charles began an irrelevant conjecture about the idea of
the commuting assassin, always catching the same train.
'Had a good day at work, dear?' 'Oh, not too bad. Had a
bit of trouble with one chap. Had to use two bullets. Still,
always the same on a Friday, isn't it?' But the situation
was too tense for that sort of fantasy.

The assassin got into an open-plan carriage, which was ideal. Charles went into the same one by another door and positioned himself in a seat from which he could see the man's leg and so would not miss any movement. He opened *The Times*, but his eyes slipped over the words without engaging or taking them in. He turned to the crossword on the principle that mental games might take his mind off the icy trickling in his stomach.

'I know that death has ten —— several doors/For men to take their exits—Webster (8).' The fact that he recognised the quotation from *The Duchess of Malfi* and could fill in the word 'thousand' gave him small comfort.

He felt ill, on the verge of violent diarrhoea. He could still see the man's leg round the edges of the seats. It didn't move, but it mesmerised him. He tried to imagine the mind that owned the leg and the thoughts that were going through it. Was the man coolly comparing methods of killing, trying to come up with another crime that could look like an accident? Had his pay-master given him a deadline by which to get Charles Paris? The word 'deadline' was not a happy choice.

Come to that, if his quarry was supposed to be in Brighton, why was he going to London anyway? Charles' fevered mind provided all kinds of unpleasant reasons. There was some particularly vicious piece of killing equipment that had to be bought in London. Or the job was going to be subcontracted and the bald man was on his way to brief another hit-man with the details. Even less attractive solutions also presented themselves.

The pressure on his bowels was becoming unbearable. He'd have to go along to the toilet at the end of the carriage.

That meant going past the bald man. Still, it might be useful to get a closer look. Charles walked past. The man did not look up.

His reading matter was unlikely for a hired killer. The *Listener* was open on his lap and a *New Scientist* lay on the seat beside him. Obviously a new class of person was turning to crime. Presumably in times of rising unemployment, with a glut of graduates and a large number of

middle-aged redundancies, the criminal social pattern
was changing.

Charles felt a bit better after he had used the lavatory,
but the face that stared at him from the stained mirror as
he washed his hands was not a happy one.

The Alfred Bostock disguise made him look seedier
than ever. The pebble glasses perched incongruously on
the end of his nose (the only position in which they
enabled him to see anything). The make-up on his jowl
looked streaked and dirty. The bright tie mocked him.
What was he doing? He was forty-eight, too old for this
sort of masquerade. What was he going to do when he got
to London? He couldn't spend the rest of his life following
the bald-headed man. The confidence that he would know
what to do when the occasion arose was beginning to
dissipate.

The journey to Victoria took just over an hour and
during that time the assassin sat quietly reading the
Listener. Charles supposed that one would have to relax
and behave normally in that line of work or go mad. His
own *Times* lay unread on his knee and no subsequent
crossword clues were filled in.

At Victoria the man got out and gave in his ticket at the
barrier. Charles tried a little detective logic. If the man
had a return ticket and yet was carrying no luggage except
his newspapers, it was possible that he had started from
London that morning, gone down to Brighton just to get
his instructions and was now returning to base. This
deduction was immediately followed by the question, 'So
what?'

The bald man walked purposefully to the Underground with Charles in tow. He bought a 15p ticket from
the machine and Charles did likewise. The man went on to
the platform for the Victoria Line northbound. Charles
followed.

They travelled in the same compartment to Oxford
Circus. The bald man was now deep into his *New
Scientist*, apparently unsuspicious.

He climbed out of the Underground station and
walked along Upper Regent Street into Portland Place.

He walked on the left, the British Council side rather than the Broadcasting House one. His pace was still even. Nothing in his behaviour betrayed any suspicion. And equally nothing in his behaviour would make any passer-by think of him as anything but a professional businessman on his way to work.

He turned left at New Cavendish Street, then right up Wimpole Street and left on to Devonshire Street. After two hours of tailing, Charles was becoming mesmerised and he almost overshot the man when he stopped.

Though they were only feet apart, the bald man still did not notice his pursuer. He walked in through the yellow-painted front door of a white Georgian house.

Charles, in a panic over nearly bumping into his quarry, walked on a little so as not to make his behaviour too obvious, then turned back and walked slowly past the house. It was expensive. Net curtains prevented snooping inside. A worn brass plate on the door—'D. M. Martin'. No initials after the name, no indication of professional qualifications.

Charles paused, undecided. It was an expensive area of London. Contract killing must be a lucrative business, if the man lived there. All around were expensive private doctors and architects. He looked up and down the road. A policeman about fifty yards away was watching him curiously.

That decided him. The Law was there to back him up if need be, and the thing had to be done. He couldn't stand the strain of being under sentence of death any longer. It was time to take the bull by the horns.

The door gave easily when he turned the handle and he found himself in a carpeted hall. The smartly suited girl behind the desk looked up at him, surprised. 'Can I help you?'

It was all too ridiculous. He had seen films about organised crime where the whole operation was run like big business with secretaries and receptionists, but he never expected to see it with his own eyes.

He was no longer afraid. Somehow here in the centre of London he felt safe. There was a policeman just outside.

He could manage. 'Did a bald man just come in here?' he asked brusquely.

'Mr Martin just arrived, but—'

'Where is he?'

'He's in his room, but do you have an appointment?'

'No. I just want to see him.'

The girl treated him warily, as if he might be important.

'Look, if you like to take a seat in the waiting-room, I'll speak to Mr Martin and see what we can do. He's got someone coming to see him at twelve, but I'll—'

'Waiting-room!' It was farcical. Charles started to laugh in a tight, hysterical way. 'No, I'm not going to sit in any waiting-room. I haven't come along with a list of names of people I want killed. I—'

The noise he was making must have been audible from the next room, because the door opened and Charles found himself face to face with the assassin. 'What's going on, Miss Pelham?'

'I'm not sure. This gentleman—'

'I've come to tell you I know all about what you've been doing, Mr Martin. There's a policeman outside and I have proof of what's been going on, so I think you'd better come clean.' Somehow the denunciation lacked the punch it should have had. The bald-headed man looked at him gravely. 'I'm sorry. I've no idea what you're talking about.'

'Oh really. Well, I'm talking about Christopher Milton and the instructions he gave you.'

The name had an instantaneous effect. Mr Martin's face clouded and he said coldly, 'You'd better come in. Ask the twelve o'clock appointment to wait if necessary, Miss Pelham.'

When they were inside, he closed the door, but Charles had now gone too far to feel fear. He was going to expose the whole shabby business, whatever it cost him.

'Now what is all this?'

'I know all about what you and Christopher Milton have been doing.'

'I see.' The bald man looked very displeased. 'And I suppose you intend to make it all public?'

'I certainly do.'

'And I suppose you have come here to name a price for keeping your mouth shut?'

'Huh?' That was typical, the feeling that money can solve anything. 'No, I intend to let everyone know what's been going on. You won't buy me off.'

'I see. You realise what this could do to Christopher Milton?'

'Nothing that he doesn't fully deserve. He may think he's a god, but he's not above the law. He is a public danger and should be put away.'

'It's that sort of small-minded thinking that delays progress. If you—'

'Small-minded thinking! I don't regard disapproving of murder as small-minded. What, do you subscribe to the theory that the artist is above the law, the artist must be cosseted, the artist—?'

'What the hell are you talking about? Who are you?'

'Charles Paris.' This was no time for pretence.

The name certainly registered with Mr Martin.

'Yes, I'm Charles Paris. I'm in the company with Christopher Milton. You know all about me.'

'Oh yes. I know about you. So it was you all the time. And now, blackmail.'

It was Charles' turn to be flabbergasted. 'What are you talking about?'

'Christopher Milton mentioned that a lot of sabotage had been going on in the show, that someone was trying to get him. It was you. And now you want to expose what he does with me.'

The voice was sad, almost pitying. It checked the impetus of Charles' attack. 'What do you mean? It's Christopher Milton who's been responsbile for the sabotage and you're the one who's done the dirty work for him. And this morning he gave you orders to kill me. Don't try to pretend otherwise, Mr Martin.'

The bald man gazed at him in blank amazement. 'What?'

'I know. I saw you in Leeds, and in Bristol, and in Brighton. I know you did it. All those early morning meetings when he gave you instructions. You are Christopher Milton's hit-man.'

'Mr Paris,' the words came out tonelessly, as if through heavy sedation, 'I am not Christopher Milton's hit-man. I am his psychotherapist.'

Charles felt the ground slowly crumbling away beneath his feet. 'What?'

'As you may or may not know, Christopher Milton has been prone in the past to a form of mental illness. He has had three or four major breakdowns, and has been undergoing treatment by me for about seven years. His is a particularly stressful career and at the moment the only way he can support the pressures it places on him is by having an hour of psychotherapy every day of his life.'

'And that's why he always has his call at ten-thirty?'

'Exactly. The hour between nine and ten is our session.'

'I see. And so you travel round wherever he goes?'

'He doesn't leave London much. Under normal circumstances he comes to me. This tour is exceptional.'

'And what happens to your other patients or subjects or whatever they're called?'

'It was only the week in Leeds when I had to be away. I commuted to Bristol and Brighton. Mr Milton is a wealthy man.'

'I see.' Money could buy anything. Even a portable psychiatrist.

'Needless to say, the fact that Mr Milton is undergoing treatment is a closely-guarded secret. He believes that if it got out it would ruin his career. I've argued with him on this point, because I feel this need for secrecy doubles the pressure on him. But at the moment he doesn't see it that way and is desperately afraid of anyone knowing. I only tell you because of the outrageousness of your accusations, which suggest that you have completely—and I may say—dangerously misinterpreted the situation.'

'I see.' Charles let the information sink in. It made sense. It explained many things. Not only the late morning calls, but also the obsessive privacy which surrounded the star. Even little things like Christopher Milton's non-drinking and unwillingness to eat cheese would be explained if he were on some form of tranquillisers as part of his treatment.

'I take it, Mr Paris, from what you said, that you overheard part of our session this morning and leapt to a grotesquely wrong conclusion?'

'Yes. I may as well put my cards on the table. I was brought into the show by the management to investigate this sabotage business.'

'If that's the case then I apologise for suggesting that you were responsible for the trouble. It seems that both of us have been victims of delusions. But, Mr Paris, why did your investigations lead you to eavesdrop on our session this morning?'

'The fact is, Mr Martin, that my investigations so far have led me to the unfortunate conclusion that Christopher Milton is himself responsible, either directly or indirectly, for all of these incidents.'

The psychotherapist did not reject the suggestion out of hand. 'I can understand what you mean—that all of the...accidents have in fact benefited him, that they disposed of people he wanted out of the way.'

'Exactly.'

'Yes. The same thought had crossed my mind.' He spoke the words sadly.

'You know his mental condition better than anyone. What do you think?'

'I don't know.' He sighed. 'I don't think so.'

'Having heard the violence of what he said about me this morning....'

'Yes, but that is a feature of the analysis situation. You mustn't take it literally. The idea of analysis is—in part—that he should purge his emotions. He says the most extreme things, but I don't think they should be taken as expressions of actual intent.'

'You don't sound sure.'

'No.'

'I mean, at the time of his first breakdown he attacked people with a knife.'

'I see you've done your homework, Mr Paris. Yes, there is violence in him. He's obsessed by his career and he is slightly paranoid about it. He does turn against anyone who seems to threaten him in even the tiniest way. I mean, I gather that the crime which provoked this morning's outburst was your falling over and getting a laugh during one of his songs.'

'An accident.'

'Oh yes, I'm sure, but he's not very logical about that sort of thing.'

'But he has expressed antagonism to most of the other people who've been hurt.'

'Yes, I'm afraid so. And a strange bewildered relief after they've disappeared from the scene. I suppose it is just possible that he could have done the crimes. You say you have evidence?'

'Some. Nothing absolutely conclusive, but it seems to point towards him.'

'Hmm. I hope you're wrong. It would be tragic if it were true.'

'Tragic because it would ruin his career?'

'No, tragic because it would mean the ruin of a human being.'

'But you do think it's possible?'

'Mr Paris, I think it's extremely unlikely. Behaviour of that sort would be totally inconsistent with what I know of him from the past and with all that I have ever encountered in other cases. But I suppose, if you force me to say yea or nay, it is just possible.'

Charles Paris looked at his watch. It was a quarter to one. In two and a quarter hours Christopher Milton had a meeting arranged on the stage of Queen's Theatre, Brighton, with the girl who had stolen the show from him the night before.

Sixteen...

THERE IS NO stillness like the stillness of an empty theatre. As Charles stepped on to the stage, he could almost touch the silence. And the fact that the building wasn't completely empty seemed to intensify the loneliness. Somewhere behind the circle people were busy in the general manager's office. In a distant workshop someone was using an electric drill. Traffic noise was filtered and reduced by the ventilation system. But onstage there was a deep pool of silence.

Len the stage doorman had not been in his little room, though he had left his radio on and was presumably somewhere around in the silent building. But he didn't see Charles enter.

It was ten to three. The stage had been preset for the evening performance after the morning's rehearsal. One light in the prompt corner alleviated the gloom. Charles stood behind a flat down right in a position from which he could see the entire stage. He looked up to the fly gallery. If sabotage were planned, the easiest way would be to drop a piece of scenery or a bar loaded with lights from above. But the shadows closed over and it was impossible to distinguish anything in the gloom.

The old theatre had an almost human identity. The darkness was heavy with history, strange scenes both on- and offstage that those walls had witnessed. Charles would not have been surprised to see a ghost walk, a flamboyant Victorian actor stride across the stage and boom out lines of mannered blank verse. He had in his bed-sitter a souvenir photograph of Sir Herbert Tree as Macbeth from a 1911 *Playgoer and Society Illustrated*, which showed the great actor posed in dramatic chain mail, long wig and moustache beneath a winged helmet, fierce wide eyes burning. If that apparition had walked onstage at that moment, it would have seemed completely natural and right.

There was a footfall from the far corner near the pass door. Charles peered into the shadows, trying to prise them apart and see who was approaching. Agonisingly slowly the gloom revealed Lizzie Dark. She came to the centre of the stage, looked around and then sat on a rostrum, one leg over the other swinging nervously. She looked flushed and expectant, but a little frightened.

She hummed one of the tunes from the show, in fact the song with which Christopher Milton had promised to help her. It was five past three, but there was no sign of her mentor.

As Charles watched, she stiffened and looked off into the shadows of the opposite wings. She must have heard something. He strained his ears and heard a slight creak. Wood or rope taking strain maybe.

Lizzie apparently dismissed it as one of the unexplained sounds of the old building and looked round front again. Then she rose from her seat and started to move gently round the stage in the steps of the dance which accompanied the song she was humming. It was not a flamboyant performance, just a slow reminder of the steps, the physical counterpart to repeating lines in one's head.

Charles heard another creak and slight knocking of two pieces of wood from the far wings, but Lizzie was too absorbed in her memorising to notice. The creaks continued, almost in rhythm, as if something were being unwound. Lizzie Dark danced on.

Charles looked anxiously across into the wings, but he could see nothing. His eye was caught by a slight movement of a curtain up above, but it was not repeated. Just a breeze.

The noise, if noise there was, had come from the wings. He peered across at the large flat opposite him and wished for X-ray eyes to see behind it. There was another, more definite movement from above.

He took in what was happening very slowly. He saw the massive scaffolding bar with its load of lights clear the curtains and come into view. It hung suspended for a moment as if taking aim at the oblivious dancing girl and then started its descent.

With realisation, Charles shouted, 'Lizzie!'

She froze and turned towards him, exactly beneath the descending bar.

'Lizzie! The lights!'

Like a slow-motion film she looked up at the massive threatening shape. Charles leapt forward to grab her. But as he ran across the stage, his feet were suddenly jerked away from him. His last thought was of the inadvisability of taking laughs from Christopher Milton, as the Star Trap gave way and plummeted him down to the cellar.

Seventeen...

THE FIRST THING he was conscious of was pain, pain as if his body had been put in a bag of stones and shaken up with them. And, rising above all the others, a high, screaming pain of red-hot needles in his right ankle.

He lay like an abandoned sack at the bottom of the Star Trap shaft. It was even darker in the cellar. He didn't know whether or not he had passed out, but time, like everything else, seemed disjointed. He remembered crying out to Lizzie, then crying out as he fell and then he remembered being there swimming in pain. There was an interval between, but whether of seconds or hours he didn't know.

He was aware of some sort of commotion, but he couldn't say exactly where. Onstage maybe, or in the auditorium. A door to the cellar opened and light flooded in.

Len was the first to arrive. The old doorman came towards him nervously, as if afraid of what he would see. 'It's all right. I'm alive,' Charles said helpfully, hoping he was speaking the truth.

'Who is it? Mr Paris?'

'That's right. Is Lizzie all right?'

'Lizzie?'

'Lizzie Dark. Onstage. There was a bar of lights that—'

'It missed her. She's all right.'

'Thank God.'

'Can you move?'

'I wouldn't like to make the experiment.'

Other people came down to the cellar. Lizzie. She looked pale and on the verge of hysterics. Some of the staff from the general manager's office who had heard the commotion arrived. So did Dickie Peck. Spike and a couple of his stage crew came from the workshop. Charles lay there in a daze of pain. He knew that he had been the victim of another of Christopher Milton's insane jealousies, but there seemed nothing to say and talking was too much effort.

They carried him upstairs. Spike and another of his men took an arm each. As the shock of the various pains subsided, it was the ankle that hurt most. It was agony when it dragged on the ground, so they lifted him up to sit on their joined hands. It still hurt like hell.

Since the dressing-rooms were up more stairs they took him into Len's little room by the stage door. There was a dilapidated sofa on which he was laid. The general manager's staff went back to phone for an ambulance. Len went off to take some tea, which was his remedy for most conditions. Dickie Peck and Lizzie Dark vanished somewhere along the way. Spike stayed and felt Charles' bones expertly. 'Used to do a bit of first aid.' His diagnosis was hopeful for everything except the ankle. Charles wouldn't let him get near enough to manipulate it, but Spike insisted on removing his shoe. Charles nearly passed out with pain.

'Spike,' he said, when he was sufficiently recovered to speak again. 'That Star Trap, it must have been tampered with.'

'Yes.'

'The locking bar was right out of position.'

'Yes, and someone had scored through the leather hinges with a razor blade. It was a booby-trap, meant for anyone who stepped on it.'

'I think it was meant specifically for one person.'

'What do you mean?'

'Never mind. You'll all know soon enough.'

'Hm?'

'Well, this sabotage to the show can't go on, can it?'

'You think it's a connected sequence of sabotage?'

'Sure of it. And after today I think a police investigation can be started. It's sad.'

'Sad?'

'Sad because we're dealing with a madman.'

'Ah.'

There was no point in hiding the facts now. It would all come out soon. 'Christopher Milton. A good example of the penalties of *stardom*!'

'So it was him all along. I wondered.' There was suppressed excitement in Spike's voice as if at the confirmation of a long-held suspicion.

'Yes.'

A pause ensued and in the silence they both became aware of Len's radio, which was still on. '... so all I can say in answer to that question is—I beg yours?'

It was Christopher Milton's voice. An American female voice came back, 'Well, on that note, thank you very much, Christopher Milton.'

A hearty male voice took it up. 'Well, there it was—an exclusive for us here in the studio on Radio Brighton—for the past half hour you've been listening to Christopher Milton live. And just a reminder that *Lumpkin!* is at the Queen's Theatre until tomorrow and it opens in the West End at the King's Theatre on November 27th. And incidentally the interviewer with Christopher Milton was Suzanne Horse.'

'Horst,' said Suzanne's voice insistently.

Spike went to turn off the radio. Too quickly. He turned back defensively to Charles. The light caught him from behind and only the shape of his face showed. The blurring marks of acne were erased and the outline of his features appeared as they must have done when he was a boy.

Charles recognised him instantly and like the tumblers of a combination lock all the details of the case fell into place and the door swung open. 'Gareth Warden,' he said softly.

'What?'

'Gareth, if Christopher Milton has just been in the

studio at Radio Brighton, he couldn't have been here tampering with the Star Trap.'

'He could have done it earlier and left it as a booby-trap.'

'And released the bar of lights to fall on Lizzie Dark?'

There was a silence. Spike, or Gareth Warden, seemed to be summoning up arguments to answer this irrefutable logic. The ambulance arrived before he had mustered any.

Len fussed around as Charles was loaded on to a stretcher and taken to the ambulance. The doors were about to close when Charles heard Spike's voice say, 'I think I'll come with him.'

The realisation of the true identity of the criminal he had been seeking seeped slowly into Charles' mind. Strangely he didn't feel afraid to have the man beside him in the ambulance.

They travelled in silence for some minutes. Then Charles asked softly, 'Why did you do it all?'

Spike's voice had lost its hard professional edge and now showed more signs of Ellen da Costa's painstaking elocution lessons. 'To show him up. To let people see what he was really like.'

'What do you mean?'

'I mean I just realised his ambitions. All he ever wanted to do was to get his own way and destroy anyone who challenged him. He was always totally selfish. And yet the public loved him. Look at the Press, everywhere—it always says *lovable* Christopher Milton. I just wanted to show the public what a shit their idol really was. All I did was to put into action what he was thinking. It was wish-fulfillment for him. Everyone who got in his way just vanished. That's what he wanted.'

'But he never actually hurt anyone.'

'But he wanted to, don't you see? He was never lovable, just evil.'

'And you hoped to bring public disgrace on him?'

'Yes.'

'But how? You must have realised that sooner or later you were going to make a mistake, commit some crime at a time when he had an alibi. Like this afternoon, for instance. He'd never have been convicted.'

'He didn't need to be convicted. The disgrace of the allegation would have been enough. Reports of the investigation would have brought up all the rows at rehearsals and showed the kind of person he really was.'

'But what made you think that there would be an investigation? The management have done everything to keep the whole affair quiet.'

'Ah, but they put you in the cast.'

'You knew I was there to investigate?'

'I was suspicious early on and when I saw you with Winifred Tuke's gin bottle, I was certain. That's why I fed you so much information, why I planted the clues for you in his car, why I told you to ask Julian Paddon about him.'

'I see.' Charles' detective achievements were suddenly less remarkable. 'Why did you hate him so much?'

'I've known him a long time. He's always been like this.'

'No, there's more to it than that. Has it anything to do with Prudence Carr?'

Spike/Gareth flinched at the name. 'What do you know about her?'

'Just that you were all three at stage school together, that she was very beautiful and talented, that nothing has been heard of her for some time, that you and he were both maybe in love with her.'

'I was in love with her. He was never in love with anyone but himself. His marriage broke up, didn't it?'

'But he wasn't married to Prudence,' Charles probed gently.

'No, he wasn't. He didn't marry her.'

'What do you mean?'

'He just took up with her, he unsettled her. He . . . I don't know . . . he changed her.'

'In what way?'

'He destroyed her confidence. He crushed her with his ego. She could have been . . . so good, such a big star, and he just undermined her. She never stood a chance of making it after she met him.'

'A lot of people don't make it in the theatre for a lot of reasons.'

'No, it was him. He destroyed her. Because he knew she

was better and more talented than he was. She stood in his way.' His words were repeated in the monotone of obsession.

'And where is she now?'

'I've no idea. But wherever she is, she's nothing—nothing to what she could have been.'

'And you loved her?'

'Yes.'

'Did she love you?'

'Yes, at first. Then he came along . . . I wanted to marry her. She refused. Said she loved him. That's impossible. There is nothing about him to love.'

'And what happened to you? Why did you give up acting? I know you started at Cheltenham.'

'My, you have done your homework. Why did I give up acting? I gave it up because nobody wanted to employ me. I'd had a good run as a child star, but it's difficult to make the break from child to juvenile. And I lost my looks, which didn't help. I developed this acne, my hair turned darker. Nobody thought I was pretty any more. I had three years of nothing. And then I thought, stuff it, I'll go into the stage management side.'

'But didn't Christopher Milton recognise you when you started on this show?'

'I don't know. I doubt it. He's totally unaware of other people.'

There was another pause. The ambulance moved slowly through the Friday afternoon traffic.

Charles began again. 'But, Spike, why? I can see that you hated him, I can see that you wanted revenge, but why do it this way?'

'I had to show him up in public for what he was,' Spike repeated doggedly.

'But the things you had to do to achieve that . . . I mean, beating up Kevin McMahon, running Pete Masters over. . . . It's all so cruel, so mean.'

'Exactly,' said Spike as if this proved his point. 'Christopher Milton is cruel and mean. That's what I had to show the public. I have seen inside his mind. That's what he would have wanted to happen to people.'

'But he didn't do it, Spike. You did it.'

'He wanted to.' The line came back insistently.

'But, Spike, people got hurt. Mark Spelthorne got killed. That's murder, Spike.'

'It was suicide. I had nothing to do with that.'

'Do you mean it?'

'Christopher Milton drove him to suicide.'

'And you didn't help him on his way?'

'No.' The answer came back so casually that Charles believed it.

'But, Spike, I still can't understand why you did it.'

'Perhaps you can't, but then you didn't grow up with him, you didn't see him use people, destroy people, always. You didn't see the smile of satisfaction on his face when someone was removed from his path. You didn't feel him all the time undermining your confidence. You didn't see him grinning with triumph every time he came out on top. He is a monster and the public should know it. Someone like that shouldn't be allowed to win all the time.'

'What do you think made him like that?'

'Ambition for stardom. He wants to be the best. Oh, I know what it's like. I was big in my teens. I was hailed as the great white hope of English theatre. I was going to get to the top. I understand the kind of pressure that puts you under. And I know that you've got to get out of it and love people, not treat them like dirt.'

'Hmm.' Charles was about to comment on how Spike had treated people but he went on on another tack. 'Do you think he's happy?'

'Happy? So long as he's on top, yes.'

So Charles told him what he had discovered that morning, how Christopher Milton could not face life without an hour of psycho-analysis a day, how he lived in fear of discovery of his weakness, how his life was split between public acclamation and private misery. 'How can he be happy when he doesn't even know who he is? His changes of mood are so violent because he has no real identity. That's why he clings to his fictional self. Lionel Wilkins is more real to him than Christopher Milton and it is only when he is in that character, hearing the adulation of an audience, that he feels alive. You hate him, you can despise his behaviour, but don't ever think he's happy. His desperate concern for his career is only because he lives through it. Take it away and you kill him.'

There was another long silence. Then Spike grunted, 'He's a bastard.' His mind couldn't cope with an idea that challenged his long-held obsession.

The ambulance swung round into the gates of the hospital. Charles felt weak. The pain in his ankle was burning fiercely again. 'The question now is,' he said with effort, 'what are we going to do about it.'

'I suppose you report me to the police.' Spike's voice was dull. 'That's presumably what the management put you into the company to do—find the wrong-doer and see him brought to justice.'

'On the contrary, they brought me in to the company to find the wrong-doer and to hush up the whole affair.'

'Ah.'

'And I don't see why I shouldn't do just that. That is, if you've been persuaded of the pointlessness of your vendetta. You cannot do worse to him than he does to himself. You cannot destroy the real Christopher Milton, because it doesn't exist.'

'So in fact you're letting me off?'

'Yes, but, by God, if anything else happens in this show, you'll have the entire police force descending on you from a great height.'

'And if I actually strike at the *star* himself?'

'I don't think you will.'

'Well, thanks.' The ambulance came to a stop and the men got out to open the back door. 'So you reckon he's a real wreck?'

'Yes. If that gives you any cause for satisfaction.'

'Oh, it does, it does.'

'What will you do—leave the show?'

'I'll have to, won't I?'

Charles was pulled out and placed on a trolley. Spike still didn't seem able to leave. He wanted to taste the last drop of news of his rival's degradation. 'So it's driven him mad. That happens. There's a danger of that with anyone who's ever been even vaguely in contact with stardom. They lose all touch with reality.'

'Yes,' said Charles, but, locked in his own world, Gareth Warden seemed unaware of the irony.

PART 5

First Night

Eighteen...

THE FIRST NIGHT of *Lumpkin!* at the King's Theatre on Thursday, November 27th, 1975, was a major social and theatrical event. Everyone was there.

Included in everyone, though less famous and glamorous than many of the rest of everyone, were Charles Paris and his wife Frances. She had somehow heard about his accident and come down to visit him in the Brighton hospital. His injuries were not too bad. Apart from extensive bruising, the only real damage was a broken ankle. In fact, the rather gloomy young doctor who dealt with him described it as a Pott's fracture and said that with a fall like that, he was lucky not to have crushed a few vertebrae, fractured his calcaneum and broken his sternum. He was out within a week, complete with a cartoon plaster on his foot and a pair of authentic-looking tubular crutches. There was no chance of his appearing in the show and there was talk of compensation from the company. The wheel had come full circle; his identification with Everard Austick was now complete.

It was difficult to say where he stood with Frances. She had accepted his invitation to the first night and there had been no mention of Alec, the scout-master. And yet she seemed distant. Perhaps just making her point that she was no longer around whenever he needed picking up out of depression. It wasn't a tangible change, but it made him feel that if really he did want her back, he'd have to work for her.

It was like going out with someone for the first time, not knowing which way the evening would turn out.

In the crowded foyer they met William Bartlemas and Kevin O'Rourke, a pair of indefatigable first-nighters resplendent in the Victorian evening dress they always affected for such occasions. 'Why, Charles...' exclaimed Bartlemas.

'Charles Paris...' echoed O'Rourke.

'What *have* you been doing to yourself...?'

'You have been in the wars....'

'What was it—some tart stamp on your foot...?'

'I don't think you've met my wife, Frances.'

'Wife? Dear, oh dear. Never knew you were married....'

'Lovely to meet you though, Frances....'

'Lovely, Frances darling. Such a pretty name....'

'But Charles, I thought you were *in* this show....'

'But obviously the leg put you out. You know what it was, O'Rourke, someone wished him luck. You know, the old theatrical saying—break a leg....'

'Break a leg! Oh, that's too divine....'

'Going to be a marvellous show tonight, isn't it, Charles...?'

'Well, of course you'd *know*, wouldn't you? I mean, you've been working with him. Such a clever boy, isn't he, Christopher...?'

'Clever? More than clever. That boy is an A1, thumping great star. If the national Press don't all agree about that in the morning, I'm a Swedish *au pair* girl....'

'Oh, but they will. He is such a big star. I think he's really brought stardom back into the business. We've had all those dreary little actors with Northern accents who spend all their time saying how they're just like ordinary people....'

'But stars shouldn't be like ordinary people. Stars should be larger than life....'

'And Christopher Milton is... so big. We were reading an interview with him in one of the Sundays....'

'By some American girl, Suzanne somebody... very good it was....'

'Oh, super. And you've been working with him, Charles. That must have been wonderful. . . .'

'Yes, but wonderful. . . .'

It was very strange seeing a show he had been with for so long from out front, but perhaps less strange with *Lumpkin!* than it would have been with anything else. It had changed so much since he last saw it that it was like seeing a new show. The cast must have been working every hour there was since Brighton. And they did well. The first-night sparkle was there and they were all giving of their best.

The show had gained in consistency of style. Wally Wilson had also been working away like mad and, for all the part he played in the final product, Oliver Goldsmith might as well have taken his name off the credits. Charles reflected that in the whole case there had only been one murder—that of *She Stoops to Conquer*.

The changes had involved more cuts and now Tony Lumpkin's part totally overshadowed all the others. In less skilled hands than those of Christopher Milton it would have overbalanced the show, but the star was at his brilliant best. He leapt about the stage, singing and dancing whole new numbers with amazing precision and that perfect timing which had so struck Charles at the early rehearsals in the Welsh Dragon Club. The show would be a personal triumph. It was bound to be if it succeeded at all, because no other member of the cast got a look in.

At the interval there was a buzz of satisfaction in the audience. Charles, who was feeling tired and achey after his bruises, couldn't face the rush for the bar and sat quietly with Frances. Greatly daring, like a schoolboy on his first date, he put his hand on hers and squeezed it. She returned the pressure, which made him feel ridiculously cheerful. Their hands interlocked and he felt the familiar kitchen-knife scar on her thumb.

He looked at the busy stalls. He could see Kevin McMahon in the middle of a congratulatory throng, smiling with satisfaction. Gwyneth, David Meldrum's assistant, was coming up the aisle towards him. They were like creatures from a previous existence.

Gwyneth stopped by his seat to ask how he was. He told her, but she hung around, for the first time in their acquaintance seeming to want a conversation. He asked a few idle questions about the company and production details. Running out of things to say, he asked, 'Who's the new stage manager?'

'New one? Why, it's still Spike.'

'Still Spike?'

'Yes, of course. He's in charge in the fly gallery tonight.'

A familiar cold trickle of anticipation crept into Charles as the lights dimmed for the second act.

It continued to go well. The audience, enlivened by their gins and tonics, seemed more relaxed and receptive. The show was building up to the climax of the Chase Scene. The profusion of comic business meant that no one was aware of the butchery that the plot had undergone. The audience exploded with laughter time and again. Only Charles Paris was silent.

The Chase Scene arrived and the audience roared. Charles held his breath when it came to the Star Trap moment, but the machinery of the King's Theatre delivered its burden safely on stage at the correct time and gained an enormous laugh.

But the respite for Charles was only temporary. He knew what was happening behind the scenes. While doubles onstage continued their interweaving and dancing, the real Tony Lumpkin climbed to the gallery where he would have the Kirby wire attached to the corset he was already wearing. The audience laughed away at the action onstage while Charles fought with the nausea of horror.

Bang on cue, Christopher Milton appeared. He descended slowly from the heavens and his appearance gathered the round of applause that always attends spectacular stage effects.

The pace of his descent suddenly accelerated. The applause died as if it had been switched off. No longer was the star coming down at a controlled speed; he was free-falling. The real panic in his eyes and the jerking of his arms and legs communicated his fear to the audience. For about twenty feet he fell and then sharply the wire was taken up again and he came to rest bobbing about five feet above the stage.

There was a long pause while Charles could feel the agony of the corset cutting under the star's arms. Then Christopher Milton pulled a Lionel Wilkins face and said, 'I beg yours?' The house erupted into laughter and applause.

And that was how the rest of the show went. Everything that should have got laughs did, every song was applauded to the echo and Christopher Milton could do no wrong. At the end there were twelve curtain calls and the audience was still shouting for more when the curtain came down for the last time.

Afterwards Charles, who was the least showbiz-conscious person in his profession, felt he had to go round backstage. There was an enormous melée of people outside the stage door.

He met one of the stage management struggling out against the crowd (no doubt sent by thirsty actors to stock up with drinks before the pubs closed). She recognised him. 'How are you? Wasn't it marvellous tonight?'

'Great. Barbara, where's Spike?'

'Well, that's strange. I don't know. He was in the gallery and then there was that cock-up in the Chase Scene. Did you notice it?'

'I think the whole audience noticed it.'

'Oh no. Apparently most of them thought it was deliberate. Anyway, Spike went off straight after that. It was very strange, he said something about some things you can't beat and that he was leaving and wouldn't be coming back. And he went. Amazing, isn't it? He always was a funny bloke.'

'Yes,' said Charles. 'He was.'

At that moment the stage door crowd surged forward and Charles and Frances found themselves swept into the theatre. Standing in the green room (he had been mobbed before he could even get to his dressing-room) was

Christopher Milton. He was smiling, radiant, happy, as the world milled around him and everyone said how marvellous he was.

He saw Charles and reached out a hand to wave across the throng. 'Hello. Are you better? What did you think of it?'

'Bloody fantastic,' said Charles. And he meant it.